Finding Laura

P.R. Hollywood

DEDICATION

IN LOVING MEMORY OF MY HUSBAND
ALAN HOLLYWOOD - 1937 - 2006
FOREVER IN OUR HEARTS AND MINDS

WITH LOVE TO MY SISTER
HEATHER RAYMOND
1944 -2021
REMEMBERING THE LAUGHTER
AND THE GOOD TIMES

CONTENTS

ACKNOWLEDGMENTS

WITH LOVE AND GRATITUDE TO MY SON
GRAHAM   J   HOLLYWOOD FOR ALL HIS HELP
INCLUDING RESEARCH FOR THIS BOOK.

WITH LOVE AND GRATITUDE TO MY NEPHEW
ROBERT EYERS FOR ANOTHER BRILLIANT BOOK
COVER AND HIS HELP WITH IT

CHAPTER ONE

'Where are you going this morning and why are you wearing that skirt? You know I don't like you making a show of your legs. Before you go out, change into some trousers.' Maxwell snarled at her.

'I'm doing what I usually do. I'm taking Mia to playschool, then calling in for some shopping. I'll come back, do some housework, go and pick Mia up and we'll come home?'

'I don't know why Mia has to go to playschool, after all she's got plenty of toys at home?'

Maxwell was looking at her straight in the eyes. He never seemed to believe anything she said to him.

'She needs to play with other children as she will be starting school soon and then she'll already know how to mix with them.' Laura stood with her eyes downcast.

'That's why we should have another baby, she would have someone to play with and wouldn't need to go anywhere.' Maxwell stood staring at her.

'Well, nature sometimes takes it's time, it will happen soon, I'm sure.'

Laura had hidden her contraceptive pills, she hated to think what he might do to her, if he knew she was taking them.

'Well, I'm off to work, make sure you are back by lunch time, I might decide to come home to eat.' Maxwell glared at her.

'I'll be home in plenty of time.' Laura breathed a sigh of relief as she heard the front door slam.

Laura rushed up the stairs and went into Mia's bedroom.

'Mia come on darling, it's time to get up. Today we are going on an adventure. I need you to hurry up and get dressed.' Laura quickly helped her daughter to have a wash and brushed her hair.

'Where are we going Mummy?' Mia said excitedly. 'Is it a surprise?'

'You'll see when we get there. Now we need to take a few of your clothes, and you can bring your favourite toy, I expect I can guess which one, it's Bunny isn't it? You always say you can't sleep without him. We are going to stay away for a few days, so that will be fun, won't it?'

Laura managed to carry the stepladder up the stairs, climbed up and opened the loft hatch.

She pulled down a large suitcase with wheels and after replacing the hatch, she quickly carried it into the bedroom and laid it on the bed.

It did not take her long to bundle a few clothes for herself and Mia, wasting no time to worry whether these would be enough.

She went into the bathroom and took their toothbrushes, flannels and anything else she thought they might need and flung them in her washbag.

She had been saving some money every week from the housekeeping that Max gave her. It had been difficult as he always wanted to know exactly what she had been buying.

She did not own a cheque book anymore, Maxwell said it was his job to look after the finances, so why would she need one?

All the money that she once had in her bank account was now in his account, so if she or Mia needed anything, she had to ask him. How had her life come to this? She had always been so independent, why did she never question him?

He had never actually hit her, but he had somehow destroyed her self-confidence. She had decided that she could no longer live this life, she thought he was controlling her every thought and decision.

She had to get away, if she did not do so now, then she never would.

Luckily, she had managed to buy some bargains and now she had saved enough money for their train tickets and a little bit more besides.

She had sold a couple of pieces of her jewellery, nothing that he had bought her of course, hoping she had enough money to get far away, the further the better.

She managed to bump the suitcase down to the front door. After making sure Mia had her favourite toy, she held her hand, while Mia jumped down the stairs.

She had a quick look around the house, making sure she had not left any clues where she was going. She put the door keys and car keys on the kitchen table but then looking down at her left hand, she pulled off her wedding ring, and placed it next to the keys.

She had decided to go by train as she was not sure whether Maxwell had put a tracker on her car. He always seemed to know, without asking, exactly where she had been.

She made one last call from her phone to the Taxi company and ordered a taxi to take her into town. She did not want the taxi driver to drop her off at the station, as Maxwell might ring them and find out where she had gone.

Without a second glance around the room, she took Mia's hand and stood waiting at the front door for the taxi to arrive, shaking with nerves that Maxwell might suddenly arrive back home.

The taxi driver put the large suitcase into the boot of the car and with a sigh of relief, Laura left the house that had become her prison for the past four and a half years.

The taxi dropped them at the shopping centre, where Laura went straight to the phone shop.

'I want the cheapest phone you have, it's just for emergency, in case I lose the one I've got.'

The salesman soon found a basic one for about twenty pounds. Laura went into the shopping mall and dropped her phone on the floor, stamped on it, then threw it into the nearest bin.

'What did you do that for Mummy? Don't you like it anymore?' Mia was obviously puzzled.

Her mother had always told her to be careful and not touch her phone.

'We've got a nice new one now, so we didn't need the

old one anymore. Right, we have got to hurry, or we are going to miss our train. You have never been on a train before so that will be exciting, won't it darling?'

They hurriedly made their way to the station. Laura had already bought the tickets a few days ago and kept them hidden. She had been terrified that Maxwell might find them.

'Let's go and buy some food for a picnic as we are going to be on the train for a long time.'

They went to a shop selling sandwiches and also bought some fruit. 'Would you like something from the cake stand, how about some buns?'

'Yes, please Mummy, can I have the ones with pink icing on?'

'Of course, you can, darling. Right, now we must hurry and find the platform where our train will be waiting to take us on our big adventure.'

They found the right platform and boarded the train, managing to find a couple of seats by the window. Mia sat watching, as the crowds of passengers began to board the train.

Mia was thrilled as it pulled out of the station and began to speed away. Laura took a deep breath, saying to herself 'Hopefully this is the start of a brand-new life. I didn't think

I was brave enough to do this but at least I know where I'm going and that there is some-one waiting to help us.'

It was far too soon to relax. It was hard to believe she had finally found the courage to escape from her tormentor.

She just hoped she would soon be far enough away so he would never be able to find her. She shuddered and tried not to think what he would do to her if he did.

CHAPTER TWO

The last four and a half years had been a nightmare. He had seemed so kind and affectionate at the beginning, she would never have imagined, it would come to this.

Laura was like any other young woman, enjoying life, spending the weekends shopping, and going to parties with her friends. How was she to know how things would turn out. If only she could turn the clock back?

Maxwell had been looking in the window of the Estate Agent's office where she had been working for a few weeks. She was enjoying her new job. It made a change from the office where she had been previously. She did not have to sit behind a desk all day and she was finding the work much more interesting.

Her new colleague Tracy suddenly said 'There's Mr.

Maxwell Hudson. I bet he is after another run down old house. He has bought quite a few of them before, with our help. He must have plenty of money because he always pays cash.

He is rather good looking and is always smartly dressed. I don't know if he is married, but I wouldn't say no if he asked me out.' Tracy laughed.

'Oh, here he comes, he must have seen something he likes the look of.

Good morning, Mr. Hudson, is there something in the window you would like the details of?'

'There's a terrace house in Blackwell Road that looks promising, have you got time to show me around? He smiled at Tracy.

'Oh, I know the one you mean, it's in a bit of a state, needs a lot of work, but that's how you like them, don't you?

I am afraid I have someone coming in a few minutes to see another house. Tell you what, how about Laura showing you around, it will be the first time she has done it on her own, so it will be good to see if she can remember all I've taught her?' Tracy smiled.

Maxwell turned and looked at Laura and at first, he seemed about to say he would rather wait for Tracy, but then he said, 'Why not, I'm in rather a hurry and if Laura would like to practice her selling technique on me, that would be fine?'

Laura looked at Tracy, she had been hoping Mr. Hudson had said he would wait for her.

'My car is parked just down the road, so we can go in that, if you like?' Maxwell smiled at her.

'No thank you, we are supposed to go in our own cars. It has got the name and number of the firm painted on the side, so it's good for advertising. I can come straight back to work after I have shown you around.

It's parked at the back of the shop, so it won't take a minute to get it.' Laura was not sure that she wanted to be driven by some-one she had only just been introduced to.

Mr. Hudson shrugged his shoulders and said, 'Right, I'll meet you there then, will you be long?'

'I will just need to get the details from Tracy, and then I'll be right behind you.'

Tracy gave her the address. 'Make sure you lock up properly after you have shown Mr. Hudson around. Don't look so worried, you'll be fine.' Tracy laughed and handed over the keys.

Laura sat in her car and put the post code into the satnav and set off for Blackwell Road. It was not the nicest part of town, but once the houses were refurbished, maybe they could be affordable for first time buyers?

The road had terraced houses down both sides and most of them looked rather worse for wear. Laura managed to park outside the number that had the 'For Sale' notice stuck to the window.

Mr. Hudson arrived in a huge shiny Mercedes and not surprisingly, could not find anywhere to park. After winding down the window, he leaned out and said, 'I know somewhere near-by where I will be able to leave my motor, I won't be long.' With that he drove away.

Laura was not sure what to do next but decided to lock her car and walk over and open the door to the house. When she tried, she had to push with all her might, as the amount of junk mail on the floor was making it difficult to open.

She managed to bend down and move some of the rubbish to one side, so she could enter.

What she saw, when she managed to get into the hall, was disgusting. The walls were covered in black fungus and smelt revolting. Obviously, the place was riddled with damp, rising from the floor to the ceilings.

She decided that before she entered any of the downstairs rooms, she would wait until Mr. Hudson had returned from parking his car.

She was glad to be able to step outside onto the pavement, and took a deep breath, happy to be out in the fresh air again.

Mr. Hudson soon arrived and said, 'I see you have opened the front door. Shall we go inside?'

'Do you really want to see this house? It's in a dreadful state, it will take an awfully long time to restore it.' Laura was not keen to go in again, the smell alone, was making her feel sick.

'I'm sure it's no worse than some of the houses I have renovated. I've got several in this road already. I have an excellent team of builders. They will have this house looking as good as good as new in no time. Come on, I'll take care of you.' He smiled reassuringly at Laura.

'Well, if you're sure? Laura said. 'You go in first, and I will follow you.'

Max pushed open the door and led the way into the front room. There was rubbish everywhere, piles of newspapers, dirty clothes and wrappers from fast food.

Suddenly, out of the pile of clothes, a mouse or maybe it was a rat, ran across the room.

Laura screamed and grabbed hold of Maxwell's hand.

'Goodness, you're easily frightened, that's nothing, all

these old houses have vermin.

We will soon get rid of them.' Maxwell patted her hand. 'Tell you what, I'll see the rest of the house on my own, you go and sit in your car.'

'If you really wouldn't mind, I think I will. I don't know what Tracy will think of me, for not showing you around?' Laura took one last look at the room, shuddered, and hastily made her way out into the fresh air.

She did not have long to wait until Maxwell reappeared. He came over to her car and smiled.

'I tell you what, let this be our little secret. Tracy doesn't have to know but what if you agree to come out to dinner with me this evening, that will make up for the mouse incident?'

Maxwell smiled 'What sort of food do you like? English, Indian, Chinese, you choose, I like most dishes.'

Laura thought Maxwell had the most beautiful brown eyes. He was obviously older than her. He was smartly dressed and completely different to the young men she usually went out with.

She sat and pondered whether to say yes for a few seconds.

'Alright, I don't mind where we go, you probably know more about the restaurants in town than I do.' Laura could not help smiling back.

'Would you mind locking up for me, Tracy said I had to make sure everything was secure?'

'Of course, I will. Just give me the keys, Tracy won't have to know.' Laura handed him the keys through the window of her car. Maxwell smiled at her and returned to the house making sure the door was locked.

Laura thought to herself. 'I can't believe that anyone would break into that hovel. There's nothing worth stealing?'

Maxwell came and stood by her car. 'So, Laura I'll come and pick you up, what about 7.30pm? I know a lovely restaurant down by the river, just give me your address and telephone number.' And that was how it all began.

He would phone her several times a day, wanting to know where she had been for lunch, what time she would be home, were there any male friends at the office? Questions, questions all the time.

He seemed to her so very sophisticated and the fact that he was older than her made her feel safe and protected. Her father had died when she was very young, and maybe she had unconsciously been looking for a father figure.

He was obviously an astute businessman, owned several houses, employing workmen to upgrade his properties.

At first, she thought that ringing her several times a day, wanting to know where she was and what she was doing, was very romantic. So, when he asked her to marry him, she quickly agreed although she had only known him for six months.

He told her he had been married before and that his wife had run away with a man she had been seeing behind his back. It had been several years ago, and he had never heard from her since.

He had been able to get a divorce as she had been missing for seven years, so now he was free to marry again.

He said because of what happened, he just wanted a simple ceremony in a register office.

However, he promised to take her on a wonderful honeymoon after the wedding to somewhere very romantic.

Laura had never wanted a big white wedding, as she had few relatives, so she was happy to have just some of her best friends attend.

The day was lovely, and afterwards Maxwell whisked her away to Venice, it was so romantic, all she had ever dreamed of. They stayed in a beautiful hotel overlooking the Grand Canal.

Life had been wonderful at the start. He was always spoiling her with presents and dinner out at the best restaurants.

Just before they were married, Maxwell sold his bachelor flat and bought a beautiful new detached house with a large garden and life seemed perfect.

However, all too soon, the coercion began, he wanted to know where she was every minute of the day. He rang the office countless times, asking who she was with, making her life a misery.

She was still working at the Estate Agents, which she enjoyed, but he kept telling her it was not necessary for her to go to work, he had plenty of money to look after her.

She nearly left him several times, but he always promised things would be better but then she became pregnant with Mia. She hoped that when their baby was born, he would change, but things only became worse.

He liked the fact that she was now at home every day. The friends she knew from the office, were banned from the house. She did suggest that she could go back to work when Mia was about six months old and put her in a nursery, but he would not hear of it.

Her confidence hit rock bottom. He was forever telling her she was an idiot and that she would not be able to exist without him. Over time she began to believe him.

He would give her money in cash each week for

groceries, and she had to keep all the receipts for him to go through so that he knew exactly what she was spending it on.

Mia was now three and a half. Laura decided that enough was enough, the time had come for her to escape, while she still had the courage to leave him.

She lay her head back on the carriage seat and looked out of the window as the fields sped by.

The more miles they covered the sooner she might begin to feel safe.

After what seemed like a lifetime, the train halted at the Main station. Mia had fallen asleep,

Laura gently woke her up.

'Come on darling, we have got to get off this train and go across the road to get on another one.'

'We have been on this train for ages Mummy. How long will it be until we are at the surprise?' Mia yawned, she was still feeling sleepy, she got to her feet and sighed.

'Not too long darling, now make sure you have got Bunny. We need to cross a very busy main road so make sure you hold onto my hand.'

Laura managed to pick up the suitcase and leaving the train, they walked the short distance across the road to the other station. Laura bought the tickets for the next train to take them to freedom.

'We will soon be at the seaside, that is the surprise! You will be able to paddle in the sea and make sandcastles. I'll buy you a bucket and spade, you'll enjoy that darling, won't you?

'That will be lovely Mummy. Will I be able to have ice-cream?'

'Of course, you will. We are going to visit your Auntie Jacky, she is my sister, you haven't met her before, so that will be exciting?'

Laura gave Mia a hug. Hopefully, life would be better for them both. She just wondered whether they were now far enough away, so Maxwell could never find them.

CHAPTER THREE

Maxwell let himself in the front door and yelled 'Laura, why haven't you been answering my phone calls, if your mobile isn't working, you should have rung me from the home phone?'

He strode into the kitchen, 'What are you doing, I want some lunch?'

He saw the keys and wedding ring on the kitchen table and stood motionless for a few seconds staring at them, then he ran up the stairs to their bedroom.

The wardrobe doors and the chest of drawers were open, and clothes were strewn about the room.

Maxwell rushed into Mia's room and the same chaos met his gaze. His face was contorted with rage as he walked back into their bedroom. He sat down on the bed and as the realization that Laura had left him and taken Mia with her, he began to laugh.

He threw his head back and smiled. 'Do you really believe that you could leave me? I will find you and bring you back. Make no mistake, you will wish you had never tried to take my daughter away from me.

You are a stupid idiot, you're not going to get away with this, haven't you learnt anything in the years we have been together?'

He stood up and walked over to the wardrobe and pulled out hanger after hanger of Laura's clothes and tore them to shreds.

He swept his arm over her dressing table and smashed every bottle and keepsake to the floor.

He began to rummage through the chest of drawers, hoping to find some letters or anything that would give him a clue as to where she had gone.

Hidden inside some underwear, he found the contraception pills. Now he knew why she had not fallen pregnant. He threw them across the room.

'You bitch, just wait till I find you. I will find you Laura, if it takes the rest of my life, I will find you.'

He rushed downstairs and went out to her car and began to search the glove compartment and the boot to see if there were any clues as to where she had gone.

He had put a tracker on her car but had checked it frequently to see if she had been anywhere unusual. He had never found anything to cause him alarm.

Where had she gone, who was she meeting? It must be a man. 'When I find him, I'll kill him.'

Laura must have been planning her escape for some time, some-one must be helping her, she did not have much money, he had made sure of that.

Where had she gone, she did not have many relatives and he had banned her from seeing any of her old friends?

Finally, when he had calmed down, he would have to think long and hard how he was going to find her, but find her he would, no matter what it cost and how long it would take.

CHAPTER FOUR

Laura and Mia had finally arrived at their destination. They had been travelling for hours and were both exhausted.

Laura remembered spending summer holidays with her Auntie Mabel in her bungalow by the sea front. It brought back many happy memories of her childhood.

Auntie Mabel and her Uncle Fred had no children of their own, so Laura and her sister were always spoiled when they stayed with them.

Hopefully now she and Mia had come many miles from her tormentor, they would be safe. She had made certain that she had never spoken of her Auntie Mabel or where her aunt lived in front of Maxwell as she had been planning her escape for some time.

Mia was nearly asleep. Laura managed to find a taxi rank and gave the driver the address. Laura's sister had said she would be waiting at the bungalow for them to arrive and that they could stay there until Laura decided what she wanted to do next.

In the mean-time Laura could help with clearing away all the clutter that Auntie Mabel had acquired over the last 60 years.

Jacky met them at the front door. She gave Laura a hug and kissed Mia. She had prepared something for them all to eat as she thought they would be hungry after their long journey. She helped to carry the suitcase into the bedroom where they could both sleep tonight.

'You must be exhausted, but I'm so pleased you finally decided to leave him.' Jacky said.

'Please don't say too much in front of Mia.' Laura whispered to her sister. 'Mia thinks we are just here for a holiday. I don't think this is the right time to tell her that we are never going back.

I will have to think of a way to break it to her gently, without upsetting her. Her father made sure he was never nasty to me in front of her, so it will be difficult to explain why we are never going back home again.'

Jacky picked up Mia and carried her into the kitchen. 'I

expect you are both hungry, come and choose what you would like to eat. There are egg sandwiches or ham, crisps and chocolate mini rolls.' Mia was soon sitting at the table and munching away on some of her favourite foods.

'I've made two single beds for you and Mia to sleep in the same room, I thought you would like to be near her in the night in case she wakes up and wonders where she is.

I will be back tomorrow, then we can have a proper talk, but I think I will leave you to have a proper rest. You must be so tired, after the long train journeys and all the worry.

The television in the front room still works but I have had the phone cut off.

You have got a new mobile phone, haven't you? So, I had better take the number in case I have to ring you in an emergency. He doesn't know about this bungalow, does he?' Jacky looked worried.

'No, I have never mentioned it or my Auntie Mabel, don't forget, he didn't want me to have any contact with my family. I just hope we will be safe here, but we will still have to be on our guard.

Thank you for all your help, I don't know where I would have gone if you hadn't got in touch and told me that Auntie Mabel had died, and that the bungalow was empty. Luckily, the letter came when he was at work, so he didn't see it.'

Laura smiled gratefully at her sister, thank goodness there was somebody who knew exactly what Maxwell had done to her over the last four and a half years.

'You know I have always hated that man. I knew from the first moment you brought him to meet me, that he was trouble, but you were so in love you wouldn't listen.' Jacky sighed.

'Please don't remind me, I was an idiot, but he was so kind and attentive at the beginning, who knew how things would turn out, not me unfortunately.

We can't turn the clock back, but hopefully now things will get better and if I can find a good job, I'll be able to make a new life for Mia and myself.'

'Good night, try to get some sleep.' Jacky went into the kitchen and gave Mia a hug and went to the front door, stopping to say, 'Make sure you lock it after I've gone and don't let anyone in, no-one knows you are here except me.

I'll see you early tomorrow morning and then we can sit and make a plan.'

'The first thing I want you to do sometime tomorrow, is help me dye my hair brown, my blonde hair makes me stand out too much in a crowd. I've managed to buy some dye, so it will be the start of a new me.' Laura kissed her sister and waved her good-bye as she walked down the drive.

As it became dark, Laura started to feel uneasy. She went from room to room making sure all the windows were locked.

The front door had a chain that she bolted and then went into the kitchen and carried a chair out into the hall, placing it under the doorknob, making sure it was secure.

Mia was nearly falling asleep, so Laura took her into the bedroom and undressed her and buttoned her pyjamas. She laid her in the single bed nearest the wall and tucked her in with Bunny.

She kissed her goodnight and went back into the lounge. She switched on the television but could not concentrate on the programmes. She turned it off and sat listening for any little sound.

She must have eventually fallen asleep, as she woke with a start. Looking at the clock on the mantlepiece, she saw it was three 'o' clock in the morning.

She thought to herself. 'He couldn't possible have managed to find me yet, I'm just being silly.'

She made her way to the bedroom and after quickly undressing, she climbed into the single bed next to Mia and managed to sleep for a few hours.

CHAPTER FIVE

Jacky arrived early at the bungalow, anxious to see her sister. She had to bang on the door several times before Laura woke and looked out of the window to make sure who it was.

She removed the chair from the handle under the front door and unlocked the chain. Jacky was looking worried. 'When you didn't answer, I thought something might have happened to you?'

'I didn't get much sleep last night, my brain was too active, going over the journey and whether I had left any clues as to where I was going. I must have finally dropped off and after yesterday I was so tired. I'm so sorry I frightened you.' Laura apologized.

'Well, you are fine and that's all that matters.' Jacky

smiled.

'Every little noise made me think, that someone was trying to get in, but eventually I did manage a couple of hours. It's going to take some time to feel safe but I'm sure I will manage it eventually.' Laura sighed.

'What's the plan for today. Have you thought what you and Mia would like to do? I have already found a playschool for her so that maybe you could get a part-time job.' Jacky went over to the sink and filled the kettle ready to make some coffee.

'I haven't told you what was in Auntie Mabel's will, have I? As she and Uncle Fred had no children, she has left the bungalow and some money in her Building Society Savings Account to be equally shared between us.

We have got to go to the Solicitors to begin to get Probate. You did bring your passport with you I hope, as you will need proof of your identity.'

'Yes, I made sure that I brought it with me, maybe Maxwell will think I've gone abroad somewhere, although I would have to get Mia a passport as well.'

Mia appeared at the kitchen door rubbing her eyes. 'Mummy I wondered where you were. Are we going to the seaside today?'

Laura went over and picked her up in her arms and

hugged her. 'Did you have a nice sleep darling, we had such a long train ride yesterday, you must have been very tired?'

'Yes, I did but Bunny didn't sleep very well. He's not used to my new bed and kept making funny noises.'

'Why was that?' Laura looked puzzled.

'I think he is just missing his bedroom and all the other toys to play with.'

Laura sighed, 'Well we shall just have to get some new ones for him to play with, won't we?

Now let's get you some breakfast and perhaps Auntie Jacky will show us the way to the shops?'

The bungalow sat right on the seafront. Uncle Fred had a loft conversion built many years ago and when the sisters had come for a holiday, they would stay in the bedroom upstairs. The view from the French windows was wonderful and there was a small balcony where they could sit and take in the all the hustle and bustle of the seaside.

It was too early at the moment for the holiday makers to be sitting on the beach in their deck chairs. The tide was out but the sun had yet to burst through the clouds.

Laura opened the kitchen window and breathed in the fresh sea air. Memories of her childhood came flooding back. How happy she had been then, nothing to worry about, just enjoying her holiday with her favourite Aunt.

They finished their breakfast and got washed and dressed. Jacky drove them to the local shops.

'Jacky, I'm thinking of changing my name. I thought of using my Maiden name, but Maxwell would know that. We will have to think long and hard what to call me. Perhaps we should just stick a pin in the telephone book?' Laura said laughing.

Jacky gave Laura a hug. 'I could kill that man for making you so unhappy and he really scares you, doesn't he?'

'Yes, he does, I don't really know what he is capable of, but I do know that he will want Mia back even if he doesn't want me. We shall have to be so careful.

I've just had a thought, has the Solicitor sent any papers about Auntie Mabel's will to my home address, if Maxwell were to open them, he would know where we are?' Laura stopped walking and grabbed Mia's hand.

'Don't worry. I didn't give the Solicitor your home address, I said you were moving down here and to address any letters to the bungalow.'

Laura took a deep breath and turned to Mia. 'I bet I know what you would like now you are at the seaside. A lovely cornet of ice-cream with a chocolate flake in it?'

They walked around the shops and bought some groceries to take back to the bungalow.

After they had something to eat, Laura said 'It's time for a new me, will you help me put on some hair dye, I think if I tried to do it myself, it would go everywhere. Goodbye blonde hair, hello the new me.'

Soon they were giggling like they used to when they were teenagers trying out new looks.

'I've certainly had lots of different hair colours over the years. Do you remember when I dyed it bright red? I looked like a pillar box. I don't know how many times I had to wash it before I was fit to be seen.' Laura laughed.

'Can I see what I look like, hand me the mirror?' She surveyed herself, twisting her head from side to side.

Mia had just come into the kitchen. She had been watching her favourite shows on the television. 'Mummy, why has Auntie Jacky put all the brown stuff on your hair, I liked it as it was, now it looks funny.'

'We just thought we would see what I would look like.' Laura gazed at herself in the mirror.

'Well, it's not the best of colours but it's certainly different, I guess I'll get used to it.'

'I expect you will need to get a little part-time job. There are lots of restaurants and cafes that need staff especially as the weather gets warmer. I could always pick Mia up from playschool for you and look after her for a while.'

'Thank you, Jacky that would be a great help. I will go and find out the times and the cost tomorrow, then I will start looking for a job, it will help to keep my mind occupied.

I keep imagining what happened when he came home from work and found me gone?' Laura shuddered.

'Well, we can make a start on clearing the bungalow, Auntie Mabel was a bit of a hoarder, the cabinets in the sitting room are full to the brim with all kinds of China.

Heaven knows where she got it all from. Of course, Uncle Fred was in the Merchant Navy and during his travels around the world, he must have brought home lots of presents for Auntie Mabel.

She hated throwing anything away, so it will take some time to clear all the rooms. If you see anything you would like to keep, maybe it would come in useful, when you get a place of your own. We will have to sort out what is going to the charity shops and what looks as if it's worth something, then perhaps we can sell it?

Not today however, we are going to enjoy ourselves, go and dry your hair and put something nice on, we are all going out to dinner.'

CHAPTER SIX

Jacky and Laura had made an appointment with the Solicitor who was dealing with Auntie Mabel's will.

Laura was feeling rather nervous about meeting him, what if he had already sent out a letter to her home address and Maxwell had seen it. He would know where she had escaped to and would soon arrive to make her return with Mia.

What he would do to her after that, she shuddered to think?

Mia had come to the Solicitors with them as they had no-one to leave her with. The Receptionist said she was quite happy to look after her while they had their meeting.

After a short while, they were called into his office. 'Please take a seat, my name is Mr. Stanton, and I am pleased to meet you both.

Your Aunt asked me to go to her Nursing Home some months ago to update her will. She and her husband had made a will before her husband died, and of course he left everything to her.

As they did not have any children of their own, she was anxious that all her estate would be left to you both in equal shares.

I just need some details about you and your sister before we can continue.'

Turning to Jacky he said 'We have had some conversations on the telephone, haven't we, but I still need proof of your identity. I did ask you to bring your passports and your national insurance number. Once I am satisfied that you are your aunt's nieces, we can begin to proceed with Probate.'

Jacky handed over her passport and national insurance number and then Laura did the same.

Mr. Stanton studied them and smiled at them both. 'Passport photographs are always very unflattering, but I can see the likeness of you both.' He smiled and handed them back.

'First of all, there is the bungalow, which I expect you will want to sell in due course?'

Jacky said 'Well we will, but we need some time to sort out our aunt's furniture, and other possessions.

At the moment we have both decided to live there for the time being. It will be easier for us to deal with all the work that has to be done. The bungalow has not been refurbished for some time so we might have to update some of the rooms before we can sell it.

Perhaps it would be best if you could tell us if Auntie Mabel has left any money for us then we could decide what we have to spend on the bungalow?'

'Your Aunt had some investments and cash in Building Societies. There is also money in her current account. I have been working out the amount when all the money has been consolidated and it comes to £100,000.' Mr. Stanton smiled at them both.

Jacky gave a little gasp, 'I didn't expect it to come to that amount of money. Bless her, she was always so kind to us when we came to stay with her in the summer holidays, when we were little girls.'

Laura had been sitting very quietly listening to what the Solicitor had been saying. 'Excuse me for asking but have you sent any letters to my last address. I am living here permanently at the moment, and I wouldn't want any of my mail to go astray.'

Mr. Stanton said, 'I didn't have your last address so any mail in the future, will be delivered to your aunt's bungalow.' Laura gave a sigh of relief.

'Well Ladies, I think that is all for the time being, I will be working on all the details we have discussed and will be in contact with you in due course.' Mr. Stanton rose and shook them both by the hand and ushered them out and called his secretary in to do some letters.

Laura thanked the Receptionist for taking care of Mia, who said it had been a pleasure.

When they went outside, Jacky said 'What did you think of that?'

'Frankly I'm amazed, I didn't think that Uncle Fred and Auntie Mabel were that well off, but I expect they were of the generation who saved their money for a rainy day.

Auntie Mabel wouldn't have been buying things every five minutes like people do nowadays, I think she was quite happy as she was, apart from buying lots of China moggies of course.' She laughed.

'This will definitely make life easier for me and Mia. When we have sold the bungalow, I think I might have enough money to buy somewhere of my own and that will be wonderful.

I just wish we could have thanked her when she was still

alive, but it never occurred to me that she would leave everything to us.'

'I'm just so happy you will never have to go back to that monster. When I think what he has done to you over the last few years. You used to be so independent, loved going out and enjoying life. This will be a fresh start for you and Mia.'

'The only trouble is that Mia loves her father, she has been saying 'When is Daddy coming to see us? It is going to be difficult when I have to explain that her Daddy won't be coming to live with us here.' Laura sighed.

'Well, we will worry about that later. The first thing is for you to make a life for yourself and after all, Mia is very young and when she starts school and makes friends, hopefully she will forget all about him.

Let's go into town and find a nice restaurant and have a celebration. We can raise a glass to Auntie Mabel, God Bless her.'

CHAPTER SEVEN

Laura and Jacky began to sort out the contents of the bungalow. It was hard work but also rather sad.

They had spent many happy times with their Auntie and Uncle when they were young children. Having to pack away all their familiar possessions was heart breaking.

Uncle Fred had been in the Merchant Navy and travelled the world bringing home presents for Auntie Mabel, from far flung places around the globe.

Most of them were obviously made for tourists such as silk fans, kimonos, brass statues of Buddha and Indian deities. A boomerang from Australia and a stuffed Koala and Kangaroo, which they both remembered playing with as children.

Of course, there were plenty of tea sets, glass vases and

model cats. Auntie Mabel had always had a cat. Usually from a Rescue Centre, a poor cat that had been mistreated or simply a stray in need of a good home.

She always kept plenty of toys for the little girls to play with, especially in the garden. There was a swing, toy prams to push their dollies around in, and of course buckets and spades to take to the beach which had all been kept in the garden shed.

Laura thought it would be nice to keep some of them for Mia to play with in the future.

As they packed away Auntie Mabel's life into cardboard boxes, they remembered how much fun and laughter they had shared.

'What are we going to do with all these things, I'd like to think some of them could go to a good home. I don't like to think of taking them to the rubbish tip.' Laura sighed, wishing she could go back to the wonderful times when she had nothing to worry about.

'Maybe we could do a boot fair? Some-body might like to buy something Auntie Mabel collected?' Jacky suggested. 'I've never been to a boot fair so it might be a laugh. We will have to arrange something.'

'I've got to buy myself an old banger to get around in, so I can earn some money. I feel bad that you are having to pay for everything.' Laura turned and looked at Jacky. 'I don't know what I would have done without you.'

'Don't be silly, you're my baby sister, you know I would do anything for you. Anyhow I have a surprise for you, come outside to the garage and close your eyes.'

Jacky led her sister outside. 'Keep your eyes closed.' She opened the garage door.

'You can open them now.' Jacky smiled as Laura saw what was inside.

'This is Auntie Mabel's car. She was still driving until a couple of years ago. She fell and broke her hip and had to have an operation. After that happened, she began to find life difficult, and she slowly became ill.

That's when I decided to move down here, after all I'm a hairdresser so I can always find work and let's face it, living here by the sea was no hardship.

I used to come and take her shopping and help around the bungalow but eventually she had to go into a nursing home. She wasn't there for very long, when sadly she passed away.' Jacky sighed.

'I wish I could have done something to help her, but I didn't know what was happening. Maxwell didn't want me to have anything to do with my family.' Laura said.

'He probably wouldn't have let me come to her funeral

anyway. I wish I could have been there for her.'

'Maybe it was just as well that I didn't get in touch with you, otherwise he would know where you are now.

Anyway, the car hasn't been driven for about two years so we will phone one of the garages and get someone to come and look at it.

It obviously will have to have a new battery and whatever else it needs to get it running.

Then we will send off the registration document and have the owner's name changed into yours. Then you will have a car of your own to get you around and you can look for a job.'

'Oh Jacky, thank you so much. I don't know what I would have done without you.?'

'It was Auntie Mabel's car, I'm sure she would be pleased to know you will be driving it. She loved this little car. She was extremely upset when she couldn't drive it anymore.'

'I can't believe how everything is working out for me, somewhere to live, money hopefully to buy a flat for Mia and me, and now a car to drive. I think Auntie Mabel must be my guardian angel.' Laura was near to tears.

'I think you're right. She must have loved us both very much.' Jacky smiled.

'Well, we had better get on with the packing, we need to clear the bungalow before we start to refurbish some of the rooms. Once we get probate, hopefully we will have some money to put towards decorating.

Thank goodness for Auntie Mabel, she has made it possible for me to lead a new life. I just hope Maxwell will never find me.'

Laura wondered how long it would take for her to feel secure from the threat of Maxwell turning up some day, that's if she ever would?'

'I could have left Maxwell sooner, if it had just been me, I would have managed somehow but, I couldn't bear to think of Mia being homeless.' Laura sighed.

'You would never have been homeless, I would always have had room for the both of you, but I know you want to have a fresh start. It won't be too long before you can buy a home of your own.

When do you think you will see a Solicitor about a divorce? You certainly had cause to leave him.

I have been looking on the internet, what Maxwell did to you is known as 'Coercive Control' and is illegal. I couldn't have put up with him as long as you did.' Jacky shook her head.

'It's difficult to say why I did, but I suppose when Mia

was a baby, I didn't have the strength or energy to do very much.

I was at home one morning after taking Mia to playschool when there was a knock at the door. I went to open it and standing there was a lady holding a little boy's hand.

It was a very cold day, and they were both wearing clothes that were rather shabby and didn't look very warm.

The little boy was coughing and looked very pale. I had never seen them before so I said, 'Hello can I help you?'

'Are you Mr. Hudson's wife? I need to see him. I've written to him lots of times, but he hasn't answered my letters.' The lady seemed very agitated.

I said 'Yes I am.' I felt sorry for them, they looked so cold, and the little boy was obviously ill. I invited them into the kitchen and made them both a hot drink.

The lady told me that she rented one of Maxwell's houses and that she had asked him time and time again to please do something about the house.

It was riddled with damp and had no central heating. Her son had asthma and needed somewhere warm to live. The rent was low and sadly, she could not afford to find somewhere better.

'I didn't know what to say but was shocked that the

house was in such a bad condition. I realized that I had never seen inside any of the houses that Max had bought to refurbish.

He always said as soon as one was finished, he had a queue of people waiting to move in.

Had he been telling me lies all this time? Perhaps he never did the work on them, only painted the walls to cover up the damp?

I asked her where the house was, and I recognized the name of the street and the number. I was just deciding I would go and see for myself what state the house was in when suddenly I heard the front door open, and Maxwell walked in.

When he saw the lady and her son, his face contorted with rage. He yelled at them to get out and she looked so frightened that she grabbed her son's hand and ran out the front door.

Maxwell slammed it after her. He strode back into the kitchen and said, 'What were they doing in my house?'

'I explained that she wanted him to do something about the damp and heating' and he just sneered at me, walked into the front room and turned the television on.

He then shouted that he wanted some lunch and that was that. He never mentioned it again. I think that was the final straw, I was seeing him for the first time, the real person I had married, and I was appalled.

I didn't know what to do. How many other people were living in dreadful conditions because of my unscrupulous husband? What could I do about it? The answer was nothing.

I was already a prisoner, but one day when I was free, I made myself a promise that I would make sure that everyone would know what he was doing.' Laura had started to cry.

Jacky came and put her arms around her. 'You weren't to know what was going on, how could you? You mustn't blame yourself.

The difference is you cared and obviously he didn't. I always thought he was nasty but now I know he is really evil.'

'I'm so afraid of him Jacky, if he can do that to people, what could he do to me?' Laura looked terrified.

'I will make sure you are safe. I'm not frightened of him. If he turns up here, we shall have to call the police. Please don't cry.' Jacky gave her a hug.

'I'm going to move in here with you permanently until we get the bungalow sold. It seems silly me paying for my flat when I want to be here with you.'

'I'm feeling much stronger now and I have vowed to myself, I will never go back to him.

Let's not talk about him anymore, let's go out and enjoy ourselves, it's a long time since I have been able to say that.' Laura smiled.

CHAPTER EIGHT

The alarm clock woke Adam from a deep sleep, he opened his eyes and peered at the clock. '5am, do I really want to do this? Sundays should be the time for a lie-in. Would it really matter if I had another hour in bed?' He groaned and pulled the duvet over his head but now he was awake, his brain would not switch off.

'What if today was the day? Wouldn't he regret not doing what he had planned last night?' He knew he would not be able to fall asleep again, so sighing he got out of bed and headed for the bathroom.

After having a quick wash and shave, he put on an old pair of jeans and jumper, pulling out of the wardrobe, the old worn jacket which he kept just for this purpose. He never dressed in his best clothes, as he wanted to keep a low profile.

He quickly had some toast and coffee and sat looking at the plan he had made last night. He decided to start with the one furthest away, then make his way back towards home.

Picking up his car keys, he went and sat in the car while the windscreen washers cleared away the morning dew, and then he set off.

After about an hour, he had reached his destination, queued up and paid his 50 pence entrance fee.

There were quite a few people here already, mainly the Traders. Adam recognized some of them as they were here most weeks. He immediately headed for the stalls at the back of the field, thinking that maybe he could find something before they did.

He began to walk around, standing for a few minutes scanning each of the tables for anything he thought could be of interest. He picked up a few items and carefully scrutinized them for flaws, hairline cracks or obvious repairs.

He always spent a great deal of time at home browsing through his collection of Miller's price guides. He found them fascinating. It was helpful to know what the average price of something would fetch, although nowadays with the Internet, it was easy for people to look up on-line to find out what something was worth, so getting a bargain was becoming more and more difficult.

Then there were the fads when something became fashionable, and the prices went sky high, only to crash and be worth next to nothing. He had been caught out that way more than once.

He stopped at one stall and saw a Clarice Cliff honey pot decorated with the crocus pattern. As he stood looking at it, an arm pushed him to one side and a Trader made a grab for it.

Adam knew not to make a comment as he would only get 'Well you should have grabbed it first,' which was true, so he made his way to the next stall.

The items for sale here were numerous and varied. Some children's clothes were hanging on a rail, and several plastic toys took up some space at one end of the table.

However, there were some interesting pieces of China and glass that Adam decided were worth checking over.

A young lady and a little girl were sitting on garden chairs behind the stall, wrapped up in blankets, against the damp chilly morning air. Adam began to scan the table to see if there was anything of interest.

There were a few pieces of China that had been part of a

dinner service, which had seen better days and some wine glasses and cheap ornaments.

Someone had obviously been very fond of cats, as there were China moggies of every shape and size.

There was nothing particularly exciting but then as Adam started to walk away, he saw a large plate which he thought might be a dish called a charger. It was in a cardboard box on the ground by the side of the table. He picked it up and it felt quite heavy.

'I put it on the ground because I thought it might slide off the table and break.' The young lady had stood up and was smiling at Adam.

Adam began to check for cracks or restoration. It seemed to be in good condition.

'Do you mind me asking where you got this from?' Adam thought it had some age to it.

'An Aunt of mine died a little while ago and my sister said that if I wanted to help clear the bungalow out, I could go ahead and keep something.

I just liked the pattern on it, I hope to buy a flat soon, but now I don't think it will go with anything. So, I thought I would bring it with me today. Also, it is very heavy, I would be frightened to hang it on a wall.' The young lady stood looking at Adam.

'Well, it looks as if it could be Chinese, there was a lot of this kind of China brought over after the Great exhibition in 1850's. It was made for the British market, they were copies of old patterns, made in their thousands. It proved to be very popular at the time. Do you want to sell it, if so, how much were you thinking of asking?' Adam said.

'I have no idea, perhaps you could make me an offer?' The little girl had now climbed up on a box and said 'Mummy, if this man buys the plate, can I have some chips from the Burger van?'

Adam grinned 'Well, let me see, I wonder how much a burger and chips will cost?'

He pretended to do some adding up on his fingers, 'What about £20, that should buy a big bag of chips.' He took a twenty-pound note from his wallet and passed it over.

'I'm sorry, I haven't got a bag big enough for the plate, but I've plenty of old newspaper, will that do?' The young lady rummaged around the back of the stall and managed to find some brown wrapping paper.

'That will be fine, I think I've seen enough of this boot fair for this morning and the Burger van is making me feel hungry, thank you very much and perhaps I'll see you again on another Sunday.'

Adam was about to pick up his purchase, when the little girl asked, 'Can we go and get some chips now Mummy?'

'Not yet Mia, we've only been here for a little while and I can't just leave the stall unattended.'

The little girl climbed down off the box and sat looking at the ground.

Adam put the plate down and looked at the little girl.

'I tell you what, I feel like having some chips myself, why don't I go and get us some?'

Adam smiled at the young woman, 'Would you like salt and vinegar on your chips?'

'Really, there is no need.' The young lady looked rather anxious.

Adam said, 'Well I'm going to have some, so it will be no trouble.'

Without waiting for an answer, Adam placed the plate back on the ground and strode off to the Burger van.

There was already quite a queue, Adam always thought that the Burger van must make more money than the stall holders, as it was always kept busy.

When he reached the front of the queue, he ordered three bags of chips and a bottle of squash.

He sprinkled the chips with salt and some vinegar. They were piping hot, so he quickly made his way back to the stall and handed over one bag to the little girl, who was now smiling broadly. 'I thought you would like a drink to wash them down,' he said handing over the bottle of squash.

'What do you say Mia?' The young lady seemed a little upset.

'Thank you very much.' The little girl sat down on the garden chair and was soon happily eating her chips.

'Well, the other bag is for you.' Adam said, handing over the chips to the young lady. 'I've got another couple of boot fairs to go to, so I will say good-bye.'

'Won't you let me pay you for the chips,' asked the young lady.

'Good gracious no, this plate I've just bought might be worth a fortune.' Adam laughed and waving good-bye, strode off back to his car.

After stowing the plate in the boot and making sure that it didn't roll around, he ate his chips and decided, to make his way back towards home and call in at another of the boot fairs that he had noted on his list last night.

After trudging around in a muddy field, getting cold, he decided he was unlikely to find anything else of interest this morning, so he decided to head for home.

He was looking forward to doing some research on the plate he had bought. He'd noticed some kind of symbols on the base, so maybe they would tell him the year it was manufactured.

After the drive home, he stopped at his local public house and decided to go in and have the Sunday roast. He chatted to the staff, and having enjoyed his meal, he drove the short distance back to his home.

He made himself a cup of coffee and settled down with his laptop and began to research Chinese pottery. There were hundreds of examples to look through, which came in all shapes and sizes. He found his tape measure and began to measure the circumference of the plate.

On the base were some strange markings, a little worn in places, but still readable.

'This is going to take me some time, so I think I'll leave it for another night.'

Stowing the plate somewhere safe, Adam settled down to watch one of his favourite shows. The Antique Road show was a must every Sunday, however, he soon fell asleep, only to wake up with a start.

He went into the kitchen and made himself some sandwiches to take to work next day. He sat reading the Sunday paper, he had left so early in the morning that he'd been unable to catch up with the news. Nothing of particular interest there, only some celebrity he had never heard of getting married and the price of houses going up.

He was saving up to put a deposit on a house or a flat. He thought, here he was, paying out a fortune in rent when he could be paying a mortgage. So far, he had managed to save a few thousand pounds but who knows when he would have enough? As fast as he could save, the prices kept going up.

He made his way to bed, sighing that the weekend was over. The morning rise at 6.30 am, would bring a week of the usual problems to be solved at the office.

Weekends went so fast, there was never enough time to do the things that he really enjoyed, but bills had to be paid, so working at a job he did not really enjoy, was not an option.

Oh well, maybe one day he would be able to give his notice in, when he found the antique of his dreams.

CHAPTER NINE

Adam had been with the same firm for several years. The work was okay but not exactly stimulating. His real love was antiques, but he knew he wouldn't be able to make enough money for it to be a full-time occupation.

Still, it gave him an interest and sometimes he did find the odd thing or two which made a small profit when he sold it on e-bay.

Of course, he always dreamed that one day he would find something worth a fortune, then he could retire and find himself a house in the country with a barn in the next field, where he could start his own antique business.

He had become quite an expert over the years and enjoyed watching the antique programmes on the television. He could sometimes recognize what the item was before the expert gave his opinion. He even knew roughly how much it would fetch at an auction.

Unfortunately, he had not made much headway finding any information about his latest purchase, the plate. He knew it was Chinese, but none of his books seemed to have a picture that was remotely the same pattern.

Some time ago, he had been to the Antique Road Show and had taken a couple of hand painted plates that he had bought at a boot fair for a couple of pounds. He had enjoyed the experience and was delighted that the expert had declared the plates were worth a hundred pounds each, which he now had displayed on the wall in his lounge.

He thought that he would take his new purchase to the show to find out the age and place of manufacture, who knows it might be worth a few pounds.

He decided to look online, to see where and when the Antique Road show was next being filmed.

Luckily, it was coming to a National Trust property, which was about an hour's drive away, in two weeks.

Adam decided that he would put in for the day off work and take the plate with him. Surely one of the experts would be able to tell him something about it that he had not been able to find on the internet or in his collection of books.

He felt quite excited. Maybe the plate could be worth

something. The experts would probably know how to find the meaning of the symbols on the underside. Maybe they were the mark of the pottery where it had been made or the potter who designed and painted it.

Soon the day arrived and covering the plate securely in bubble wrap, he drove to the National Trust Property where the filming was taking place.

There were crowds of people queuing, waiting with their treasured possessions, hoping that they had something that was going to be worth a fortune.

The grounds had been taken over by the television crew. There were tables dotted around with large umbrellas covering them in case of rain or too much sunshine.

Each table had two chairs for the Experts to sit and examine the antiques that the public had brought along to be valued.

Adam was directed to a central desk where he was asked to show the item he had brought and was told to join the queue for Ceramics. This queue was extremely long, so he knew he would have a long wait.

He supposed that most people had some sort of China, that had been passed down through the family, and were hoping it was an heirloom worth a great deal of money.

The people in the queue were soon talking to each

other, showing the person next to them, what they had brought along to be valued.

A lady in front of Adam, turned around and asked, 'What have you got in that large bundle of bubble wrap?'

'Well, I don't know, that's why I'm here today because I can't find anything similar on the internet.' Adam smiled politely.

'Would you like to see what I've brought?' Without waiting for an answer, she started to unwrap from her shopping bag, a couple of China dogs with chains around their necks.

'My mother always had these on the mantlepiece at home and when she passed on, she left them to me, I would imagine they are quite old don't you think?'

Adam looked at them and said, 'Have they got any sort of damage such as chips in the China or cracks, that would reduce their value?

'Oh goodness no, Mother wouldn't let anyone dust them but herself. I think they had belonged to her mother, so do you think they are very old?'

'Well, I can see that they are a pair as they are facing each other, sometimes people think they have a pair, but they are not, as they are facing in the same direction.

I think they are Staffordshire flat backs, so called

because no one would see their backs on the mantlepiece. The backs were not usually decorated. They look quite old, I would say, somewhere around 1840. Their value would be around £200-220 in good condition.'

'Good-gracious, as much as that? My children think they are ugly and have said that they don't want them when I'm gone. Do you think I should sell them?'

'You could put them in an auction, but you would have to pay a percentage to the auction house as well as V.A.T, but if your children aren't interested then you might as well sell them and buy something you would like.'

'Thank you very much, young man. You do seem very knowledgeable. I don't really need to see the expert now, do I?' She smiled and started to wrap the China dogs up and put them back in her bag.

'Oh, please stay in line, I may have got it entirely wrong.' Adam laughed.

The queue slowly made its way and after a long wait, Adam arrived at the table where the two experts were sitting. Adam was beckoned by one of them to come and sit down.

'Let's see what you have brought to show us today.' The expert sounded rather weary, which was not surprising, when the queue of people waiting to see him was so very long.

Adam carefully unwrapped the plate from the bubble-wrap and placed it on the table.

The expert looked at the plate and carefully turned it over. He reached for a magnifying glass and started to study the markings on the back. He seemed to be taking his time. He picked up a large book and began to thumb through the pages.

Adam sat watching as the expert turned page after page. He then asked his colleague to have a look and they muttered a few things to each other.

Finally, the expert said to Adam. 'Would you be prepared to wait for a while in the house, they will take good care of you. There are some refreshments, I expect you could do with a drink, I know I could. I just need some time to do some more research on your plate, is that ok?'

Adam said of course he wouldn't mind, and shortly after one of the helpers took him into the house and brought him a cup of coffee. Several other people were sitting in the big hall. A lady next to Adam said 'This is exciting isn't it. Are they going to film the item that you have brought in today?'

'I don't know, they just said they wanted to do some more research. What about you, do you know if they are going to film you?'

'Well, I've brought a large piece of furniture. What I mean to say, is that someone came to the house a few weeks ago, to look at a cabinet which my uncle left me.

I had written to the Road Show about the cabinet, and they said after studying it, they would be prepared to bring it here today. Obviously, I said yes, there is no way I could have brought it here myself,' she laughed.

'It will be interesting to hear what they say about it. I'm not sure what time they are doing the filming, I suppose it depends on what else they find today?'

Adam nodded in agreement and then decided to shut his eyes, lean back in his chair and pretend he was having a little nap. His brain was racing. Perhaps the plate was really old and rare.

It could be worth a lot of money. This was what he had always dreamed of, but he took a deep breath and tried not to get too excited.

After what seemed forever, one by one the people waiting in the hall were called to go outside and filming started. When the experts pronounced how much each item was worth, Adam could hear the crowd clapping.

The lady next to him was called, she stood up and turned to Adam, 'Well wish me luck, hopefully it will pay for some of the children's university fees in the future,' she laughed.

Adam, by this time was feeling rather nervous, 'The plate is probably just a copy, and they want to film it so that people aren't duped into paying a fortune for a plate like mine.' He thought to himself. 'I've seen that happen before on the show, people's expectations are raised only to be dashed again.'

In time the hall was nearly empty, Adam thought that he had been forgotten so he went and asked one of the helpers if he would be able to go home soon.

'No one has forgotten you sir. I believe that it has taken some time to find the details in order for the expert to make the right valuation. I think they have nearly finished filming the other items and that you will be next.'

Soon after, Adam was taken out into the garden. His plate was now on display on a table covered in a white cloth. The expert welcomed him back. A small crowd of people were standing around waiting for the filming to begin.

'I have had to do some delving into my book on Chinese pottery and I'm pleased to tell you that I eventually found your plate.' The expert began.

'Most people assume that Chinese porcelain is blue and

white. However, the plate that you brought to us today is from the Kangxi period, which was 1662-1722. It would have belonged to a very wealthy personage maybe one of the emperors.' The crowd let out a gasp.

'Would you mind telling me where you got it from?' The expert stood waiting for an answer.

Adam's mouth had suddenly become rather dry. 'I bought it at a boot fair about four weeks ago. I tried to find out what dynasty it was from but with no success.'

'Would you mind telling me how much you paid for it?' The expert asked.

Adam thought the expert was building up the suspense in order, to tell him it was a cheap copy.

'Twenty Pounds.' Adam was finding it hard to breath.

'Well, you certainly got a bargain, a plate similar to yours, and this one is in better condition, sold at auction a short while ago,' the expert paused dramatically, 'For Thirty Thousand Pounds'.

The crowd behind them gasped then began to clap.

'Well, sir what do you think of that?' The expert smiled at Adam.

Adam felt rather dizzy, he looked at the expert, 'Are you absolutely sure that you have the right plate? I can't believe it's true, would you tell me where you found it as I did some research but couldn't see anything remotely like it.'

'Luckily, I remembered I had seen something similar at an auction for Chinese pottery not long ago. The Chinese seem to be anxious to buy back some of the antiquities that have been sold around the world, that is why they are paying such huge prices.' The expert smiled at Adam.

'I'm rather shocked and upset that I only paid twenty pounds for it.' Adam managed to say.

'It's not your fault that the person you bought it from didn't know it's worth and after all, neither did you. There really is no need to blame yourself, finders-keepers, as they say. I would just enjoy it.' The expert smiled reassuringly.

'That's true, but I think if I do sell it, I would feel better, if I could find the young lady that I bought it from and give her some of the money.'

'Well, that's very commendable of you and I hope you find her. You have certainly made my day. I can't remember when I last saw a plate like yours. Thank you very much for bringing it along.' The expert seemed anxious to finish filming.

'Would you mind telling me when this episode of the Antique Roadshow will be shown on the television?' Adam thought that if the young lady were to see it, maybe she would come forward, and explain it was she who sold the plate to him.

'Would it be possible to film me asking for her to get in touch, maybe you could give her my address'.

'We film the roadshow months in advance, the ones that will be shown shortly on the television, were filmed last summer. I don't think that would help you to find her.

You are really worrying too much about the price that you paid for the plate. Just enjoy your good fortune, I would'. The expert smiled at Adam.

They both shook hands and a helper picked up the plate and took Adam back into the house. Adam was in rather a daze but wrapped the plate up and was about to make his way back to his car when someone tapped him on the shoulder.

'Excuse me sir, my name is John Haynes. I am a reporter from the local newspaper. I was listening while you had your plate valued and I must say I was amazed how much it was worth.

However, what struck me was your reaction to the price and that you wished you knew the young lady who sold it to you.

If you would consider having a short story printed in our paper with a picture of you holding the plate, maybe the young lady would come forward. What do you say, is this something you would like to do?'

Adam was still finding it hard to believe what had just happened but what the reporter had just suggested seemed to make sense. How was he going to find the young lady on his own?

He would obviously go back to the boot fair to see if she was there again but that might take months. It might have just been a one off that day, when she had decided to sell a few things.

'Well, if you think it might help, perhaps I would be willing for you to print the story. Surely if she did see the plate in the paper then she would remember what happened that day?'

Adam really did feel uncomfortable about the price he had paid and kept thinking about the little girl, perhaps, they might really need some money, after all that is probably why they were at a boot fair.

'Well, first things first sir, what is your name?' The reporter got out his notebook and pen.

'Adam Marsh. I live about an hour's drive away from here.'

'Do you often go to boot fairs to find a bargain? Asked the reporter.

'Yes, it's a hobby of mine, but I have never found

anything that was worth as much as this piece of China. It was always a dream of mine that I would, but I am still finding it difficult to believe what has just happened today.'

'Can you remember anything that would help us find this young lady, her hair, how tall she was, did she have anyone with her to help on the stall?' The reporter was writing everything down in his notebook.

'She had long brown hair, and was about 5ft 5inches tall, I think. She had a little girl with her, I do know the little girl's name, because her mother called her Mia.

I bought them both some chips from the burger van to say thank you for the plate, it now seems such a trivial thing to have done, but at the time I really didn't know how much the plate was worth.' Adam sighed.

'Well, that should help knowing the little girl's name, someone might recognize her. All we need now is a photograph of you holding the plate.'

The reporter helped Adam unwrap it and asked him to stand outside the hall. The light was beginning to fade but after a few attempts, the reporter thought he had a good enough image for the paper to print.

'How are you going to ask who ever sold it to me to get in touch, I don't really want to give you my address to print in the paper?' Adam was not sure he wanted anyone to know his address now he had such a valuable antique. He would have to decide what he was going to do with it.

'What I would suggest when writing the item, if anyone has any information, they send a letter or an e-mail to the paper and we will forward it on to you, that way your address will not be needed,' said the reporter

'That sounds like a good idea, of course you will have to know where I live but I would like to be sure that you do not pass it on to anybody without my consent. When do you think it will be in the paper?'

'Well, it's Wednesday today so I think it will make Saturday's paper, some people now only buy the papers on a Saturday to see what's happening in the local towns and what's going to be on the television for the next week.

Can you write down your address on this piece of paper? I promise you that it will not be printed.' The reporter handed Adam a pen and paper.

'I hope she sees it, but I will also be trying to find her myself. I know lots of people would not care about the person they bought it from, but I don't think that this lady and her little girl had much money, and I won't be happy until I can find her.' Adam shook the reporter's hand and made his way back to the car.

He made sure that the plate was secured in the boot and

drove home. He let himself into his flat and tried to decide where to put the plate for safekeeping.

His brain was buzzing with thoughts of what had happened today, and he was sure he would not get much sleep tonight.

He would have to decide what to do with the plate, something so fragile could easily be broken. He wrapped it in a large towel and hid it in the blanket box in his bedroom.

He made himself some supper and watched some television, but he couldn't concentrate on anything.

He got ready for bed and spent a sleepless night worrying about the young lady and her little girl.

CHAPTER TEN

Adam bought a copy of the paper that the reporter worked for. The reporter had got in touch to say that the story would be printed on Saturday on the front page. Adam read it and looked at the photograph of him holding the plate.

Surely someone would come forward when they saw the amount of money that the plate was worth. Although now he knew how much it would make at auction, he would have to decide what he was going to do with it.

The Editor thought it would make people smile that a young man could be so generous, as to want to share his good fortune with the young lady he had bought the plate from at the boot fair.

Soon several other papers got in touch wanting to speak

to Adam and he became quite a celebrity. So far there had been no response to his plea for the young lady to come forward.

Adam had decided to have a day in London to take the plate to a famous auction house. He had sent them an e-mail with a picture.

He had explained that the plate had been filmed and valued by a ceramic expert at the Antique Road Show who had valued it at £30,000. pounds.

He had decided he wanted a second opinion before he made the decision to put it up for sale. Having something so valuable in the house was rather worrying not knowing where to store it to keep it safe.

He had been back to the boot fair where he had bought it from and retraced his steps to the place where the young lady's stall had been.

There was no sign of her and although he walked around the whole of the fair looking everywhere, she was nowhere to be seen.

He did stop and enquire if anyone knew who she was, but to no avail. His only hope was now the picture of the plate had been in several papers, that she or someone who knew her, would get in touch.

Of course, a few people at work had seen the article in

the papers and laughingly asked him if he was going to retire, but most people wished him luck and said they would have to start going to boot fairs on the off chance of finding something as valuable.

Adam thought it was strange that no one had come forward but just as he was about to give up hope, John Haynes from the local paper got in touch.

'Is that Adam? I've got some news for you. Today we have received a sealed letter addressed to you. Let's hope it is from the young lady you are trying to trace.

That would make a wonderful follow-up story. Everyone is waiting to see who the lady is and her reaction to the good news.'

'That's wonderful, did she post the letter, or did she just pop it through the letter box, that could mean she doesn't live very far away.' Adam wasn't sure how he would feel when he finally got to meet her again.

'It was obviously delivered by hand, no stamps, or forwarding address on the back of the envelope. Will you be able to pick it up or do you want me to send it to you?

'I'll pop in on my way back from work, if that's alright, I will bring it home to read and then let you know if this is the right lady. Someone could be pretending to be her I suppose, hoping to get their hands on the money?' Adam laughed. 'Right, I'll see you later, finger's crossed, she's the right one.'

CHAPTER ELEVEN

Adam called in at the newspaper offices on his way home from work. He was excited to read the letter that had been left for him. It would be good to find the young lady before he took the plate to the Auction House in London.

'Hello, I'm Adam Marsh, I believe you have a letter for me?' Adam smiled at the receptionist.

'Good afternoon, nice to meet you, I've been following your story in the paper, I hope it is good news and that you have found the young lady, it's quite romantic, isn't it?' The young lady smiled back.

'Well, I don't really know her, I only met her for a few minutes, but it will be very nice to speak to her again.'

The receptionist rang for the reporter 'John, Adam Marsh is here.' John said something to her.

'John says, he won't be a minute. You will let us know what happens won't you, we're all really excited to see how everything turns out.'

John soon arrived at the front desk clutching the letter. 'Hello Adam, glad to see you.

Well, here is the letter, it's handwritten, something you don't see very often. I was tempted to steam it open, only joking of course.' He laughed, passing it over to Adam.

'Thanks, if you don't mind, I want to take it home and read it in private, you don't know there might be something she doesn't want spread all over the papers.'

'How intriguing, that would make the story very interesting, if the letter contained something of a mystery.' John laughed.

'Well, we shall just have to wait, I will get back to you once I have had time to consider the contents, many thanks for your help.'

Adam made a quick departure. He was in a hurry to get home and read the letter. He drove the short distance, impatient to see if this was really the young lady he had been looking for.

On reaching home, he didn't wait long to tear open the envelope and begin to read the contents.

Dear Mr. Adam Marsh,

I was shocked to read the article in the local paper concerning the plate I sold you at the boot fair.

I am very glad for you that it turned out to be such a valuable antique. Obviously, I had no idea, but I'm sure, neither did you?

You will probably think this is strange, but I do not want to come forward, to collect my share of the money. In fact, I would be grateful if this was the end of the stories being printed in the newspapers.

I will not go into details, but you could be putting me and my little girl in great danger.

Perhaps you could make up something to tell them at the newspaper office, that I have gone abroad and relinquish all rights to the plate and just wish you well.

Please do this for me. I would be very grateful.

Thank you,

The lady at the boot fair.

Adam read the letter, then read it again. Now he was not worried about giving the lady the money, he was just worried about her!

What had he started? He would never have let the press get hold of the story if he had known it could have caused harm to her and her little girl.

His thoughts returned to the morning of the boot fair,

nothing seemed to be unusual. Obviously, the only reason Adam could think of, was the lady didn't want someone to know where she was.

Who could she be hiding from? He felt responsible for the situation he had unwittingly put her in. What if the person found her due to the newspaper articles? He would never be able to forgive himself.

Now he would not feel at ease till he knew for sure that she and her little girl were safe.

He would have to find her to put his mind at rest, knowing for himself, that she was not in danger. How to go about it? She couldn't live very far away, as the letter had been posted by hand through the newspaper's letter box.

His only hope was to retrace his steps back to the boot fair, surely someone had spoken to them during the day. A mother with a young child, would surely stay in someone's memory?

That is what he would have to do, but the first thing, was to stop the papers printing anymore stories about her.

She had suggested that he tell them she had gone abroad, this was obviously to stop the person that she was frightened of from finding her address.

He put the letter back in its envelope and made his way back to the newspaper offices, the sooner he did as she asked, the better he would feel.

He asked at the Reception Desk if he could have a word with John Haynes. John soon appeared and smiled at Adam 'Well is it her, have we found the right lady. This is going to make such a good story. Everyone has been asking about her?'

'Yes, it was her but I'm afraid she doesn't want any more publicity, she is quite happy for me to keep all of the money. She said she had no idea the plate was worth so much but that neither did I.

She is about to go and live abroad, and as far as she is concerned, she wishes me well and hopes the money will come in useful for something in the future.'

John sighed 'How annoying, I was going to do a special photo of you both for the front page.

Are you really sure she is the right lady? It seems strange that she was selling some of her possessions at a boot fair. You would think she would be happy to know that she would be entitled to a share of £30,000.' John was annoyed that the story would not have the happy ending that he had envisaged.

'I'm sorry but she was adamant she didn't want me to do any more publicity, so if that's what she wants then I have to abide by that.' Adam wanted to bring the conversation to end. He did not want to discuss it anymore with John.

'I'm sorry to have brought this news as I know you were as excited as I was when the letter arrived, but I suppose it is good news for me, I get to keep all the £30,000 pounds,

If you want, just put a short item in the paper to say that the lady has been found but is going abroad and wishes me good luck.'

John sighed and said, 'Well it's not the story I was hoping for but as you say, if that is what the lady wants, then that's what I will have to do.'

He shook Adam by the hand and said he hoped he would be able sell the plate and joked that he would have to start going to boot fairs.

Adam went outside and stood for a while thinking what to do next. He felt relieved that John had not pressed him for any more information about her but still felt he wouldn't be happy until he had found her.

There was nothing he could do till Sunday morning, when he could begin his search.

He wished he had never found the wretched plate. It was only bringing him trouble and worry.

CHAPTER TWELVE

Adam decided to return to the Boot Fair where he had bought the plate, he had been there before but perhaps someone would remember seeing the young woman and her little girl.

He had not been able to sleep last night, he kept remembering what the letter had said, that he might have put her in danger.

How he wished he had not agreed to have the story printed but he was not to know that what he was doing could have such a dreadful effect on some-one's safety.

He was determined to do everything he could to find her and try to help with whatever was scaring her. He felt so responsible for the publicity in all the papers, but he had just wanted her to have a share in the money from the plate.

Sunday could not come quick enough, he rose early, and drove back to the fair where he had bought the plate.

He arrived at the field just as everyone was unpacking the goods that they had come to sell.

This time, he went to all the tables and asked whether they knew who the mother and the little girl was. Some of the people recognized him from the papers and were only too happy to talk to him.

Most of them said he was a very generous young man to want to share the money but had no information to give him as to the whereabouts of the young lady.

He was just beginning to think he was on a wasted journey when a lady on a stall which sold mainly children's clothes said 'I think her daughter goes to the same playschool twice a week as my little girl. You said her name was Mia.

Her Aunt Jacky comes to pick her up after school as her Mummy sometimes works in the afternoon. I have spoken to each of them as we wait for the children to come out.'

Adam was overjoyed and explained why he wanted to see her. She laughed and said, 'I wish someone would come and give me some money then I wouldn't have to get up at 5.30am on a Sunday morning to do this Boot Fair. She's a very lucky lady to have sold her plate to you.'

'Do you know where she lives. I know the little girl's name is Mia, but I don't know the name of her mother?' Adam breathed a sigh of relief that he might actually be able to find her.

'I think her name maybe Laura, but if I tell you where the playschool is, maybe one day you can go there and wait for Mia to come out. My little girl goes there on Tuesdays and Thursdays and that is when Mia is there, I hope you find her.'

Adam wrote down the address, and thanked the lady profusely, saying he would have to have a day off work, but it would be worth it if he could finally give the young woman and her little girl, the money for the plate.

He gave the lady on the stall five pounds to buy herself something and waved goodbye as he made his way back to his car.

He knew it would not be any use going to find the playschool today. He would have to wait until next week when he would have a day's leave on Tuesday to see if Mia came out of school and her mother would be waiting for her.

He would have to be careful not to scare her, that was the last thing he wanted to do. He would have to think long and hard how he would approach her.

He would need to tell her he had done as she asked and stopped the paper from printing anything else about her and the plate.

He drove home much relived that he would finally be able to find them both. The words in the letter were still playing on his mind.

What if whoever she was hiding from had found her, he would never forgive himself. Hopefully now the publicity had stopped, she would be feeling safer.

CHAPTER THIRTEEN

'Look who's staring in the window, it's Mr. Maxwell Hudson. I hate that man and to think I was the one who introduced Laura to him. Here he comes looking for another broken down old wreck.'

'Good morning Tracy, it's such a long time since we last met, how are you?' Maxwell smiled at her.

'I'm fine thank you. How is Laura and Mia?' Tracy didn't smile back.

'They are both very well. They have just gone off for a little holiday with her sister Jacky. I think you met Jacky at our wedding. Did you manage to talk to her?'

'I can't remember, it's rather a long time ago.' Tracy wondered why he was asking her this question.

'Laura has very few relatives, her father died when she

was very young, and sadly her mother died of cancer a few months before our wedding. It's good she keeps in touch with her sister Jacky.' Maxwell was staring at her.

Tracy didn't speak for a few seconds then said 'I haven't really had a chance to talk to Laura for a very long time.

I used to see her at the shops occasionally but whenever I said, 'why don't we go for a coffee and a chat? she would always say she was in a hurry and had to get back home.' Tracy raised her eyebrows and stared back.

'Oh well I expect she needed to pick up Mia from playschool and had things to do before that.'

Maxwell was making Tracy feel extremely uncomfortable, he obviously did not believe a word she said.

'Well, is there anything in the window today that you are interested in, if not I have rather a lot of paperwork to sort out?' Tracy was hoping he would just leave.

'Not really, I already have enough houses to rent, I don't really need to buy anymore at the moment.' Maxwell said, the expression on his face was making Tracy feel quite scared.

She wondered why he had come into the office if he had no intention of buying something.

'Well, when you talk to Laura next, please give her our

love and say that we would like to meet up after she comes back from her holiday.' Tracy was hoping to bring this conversation to a close.

'Yes, I will certainly do that, good morning.' Maxwell turned and strode out of the door.

'Well, what do you think that was all about?' Tracy sat down at her desk. 'That man gives me the creeps. He seemed to be trying to find out something about Laura's sister.

I wonder if he thought I knew Jacky's address. Even if I did, I wouldn't give it to him.' Tracy paused and sat thinking to herself.

'Wow, I've just had an idea, what if Laura has finally had enough and she's run away?

Good on her I say, but he is such a horrible man, it must have taken such a lot of courage to do that. I just hope he never finds her.

He told Laura that his first wife had run off with a man she had been seeing. No one ever heard from her again. If he treated her like he treats Laura than I'm not surprised she ran away.'

Tracy wished she did know where Laura's sister Jacky lived. She could have telephoned her and found out if Laura was staying with her, just to put her mind at rest that she and Mia were safe.

She did know that Jacky was a hairdresser as she had styled Laura's hair for the wedding.

Tracy did have a few words with her before the ceremony and Jacky had said that she was not happy that Laura was marrying Maxwell. She thought he was far too old for her and seemed to want to control everything she did.

Tracy could not remember any of Maxwell's relatives at the wedding, his best man was a builder who worked on the houses that Maxwell bought.

She did think at the time that it was rather strange that he did not seem to have any friends to invite.

Tracy just wished she knew whether Laura and Mia were safe, miles away from the man who had controlled her every move for the last few years.

'I hope he doesn't find her. He has made her life a misery. I don't know how she has put up with it for so long. I say good luck to her and her little girl.

I don't think I shall get much rest tonight. I shall be worrying what has happened to Laura. Who knows what that man is capable of?'

CHAPTER FOURTEEN

Adam got into his car and sat for a few moments trying to decide how he would approach Jacky or Laura without frightening them.

He really did not have a plan. He would just have to see when he got there what was the best way to approach them.

He started the car and drove off towards the seaside town where the lady at the boot-fair told him he might find Laura.

While driving he kept rehearsing in his mind what he would say. 'Hello, do you remember me? I'm the person you sold the plate to.' He sighed, that certainly would not do.

'Please do not be upset, no one is with me. I told the reporter you have gone abroad, as you asked me to.'

Maybe that would be a better way to approach her? What if it was her sister Jacky who was picking up Mia today? He had never met her although she might have seen his picture in the paper, obviously Laura had.

The nearer he got to the town, the more stressed he became. Laura was obviously scared of someone, Adam did not want to frighten her, after all if he could find Laura, maybe so could the person she was so afraid of.

He reached the town and found somewhere to park. Looking at his watch he saw he had plenty of time before the children came out of the playschool at 3.30pm.

He decided to walk along the high street and turn down one of the side streets and onto the beach. Maybe a walk along the sea front would settle his nerves.

He had been to this town before but that was several years ago. There had certainly been some changes since then. There were more shops, several new houses had been built and the whole town had taken on an air of prosperity.

When he reached the beach, he could see that there was a Marina with shiny new yachts bobbing about on the water. Maybe that was why the town had taken on an air of affluence.

Maybe people with money were coming down from London to spend time in the town and perhaps they were buying second homes.

He came to a well-known fish restaurant that he remembered was famous for oysters, he was not a fan, a nice fillet of salmon or cod was more to his liking.

The restaurant also had a bar, so he decided to go in and have a drink to steady his nerves. The place was packed, it was obviously very popular, most seats and tables were already taken.

He sat down on a stool at the bar but instead of having an alcoholic drink, he decided on a coffee. He ordered one and sat looking around the room.

He was still trying to make up his mind how to approach Laura. Should he follow her home, no, that really would scare her. He dismissed that thought immediately. He finished his coffee and decided to walk further along the beach, maybe the sea air would calm him down.

As he was walking along, he kept thinking, perhaps if he found out where she was living, maybe sending a letter would be the wiser thing to do, but then she might think he was stalking her.

He looked at his watch, the playschool would be closing in 20 minutes time, so he decided to make his way back there and see how he felt when the children came out.

He reached the road, where a crowd of people were

waiting at the gates of the school.

Adam quickly joined them, standing at the back where he couldn't be seen.

He heard a bell ring and shortly after the double doors to the school opened. A teacher was standing at the front making sure that the children did not run down the steps.

Parents were waiting until they could see their children and then came forward to give them a hug.

Adam stood waiting to see if he could recognize anyone and then he heard a voice call 'Mia, and there she was, Laura.

She bent down and scooped her daughter into her arms and hugged her. Mia was carrying a piece of paper which Adam could see was a drawing. Laura set her down and took her hand and they both started walking towards the car park.

Adam followed at a discreet distance. He was still undecided what to do.

Laura and Mia reached a small white car, when suddenly Mia dropped her drawing and a gust of wind blew it across to where Adam was standing, he bent down and managed to catch it.

He stood still for a few seconds wondering what to do, then walked across to the car.

'Here you are, you nearly lost it.' He bent down and gave the picture back to Mia.

'What do you say Mia?' said Laura.

'Thank you.' The little girl smiled at Adam.

'You're very welcome.' He smiled at Laura who was about to turn and open the car door when she stopped and stared at Adam.

'It is you isn't it, Adam Marsh. What are you doing here, have you brought a reporter with you?' Laura looked as if she was about to burst into tears.

Adam immediately reassured her, 'No one is here with me. I was so upset when I read your letter that I just wanted to make sure you were safe. Please believe me no one knows I'm here.'

Laura turned to Mia. 'Get in the car darling, I'm just going to have a talk to this gentleman for a few minutes. It's cold out here, I won't be long.' Laura helped Mia into her car seat.

'How did you find me, have you told anyone else where I am?'

'I went back to the boot-fair several times trying to see you and then the other week a lady I spoke to said that her daughter went to the same playschool as Mia. I just wanted to know that you were ok. I didn't mean to scare you.'

Adam said.

'If there is anything that I can do to help you, please tell me. All I wanted was to give you half the money from the plate. I have taken it to an Auction House in London who are shortly having a sale of Chinese Ceramics and I decided to leave it there until the sale.

I didn't like having something so valuable in the house so I thought it would be safer.

I am so sorry about the publicity, but I thought I was doing it for the best. How was I to know that I was putting you in danger? If I had, I would never have let the papers print the story, please believe me?'

Laura stood looking at him for a moment 'I do believe you, there are not many people who would want to share their good fortune with the person who sold them such a valuable item at a boot-fair. You are absolutely sure no one knows you are here?'

'Well, I suppose the lady at the boot-fair who told me about the playschool might ask you if I had been to see you, but you could just say no.' Adam sighed, perhaps this had not been such a good idea after all.

'If I were to tell you who I am hiding from, do you promise not to tell anyone?' Laura believed Adam had been telling the truth.

Perhaps if he knew her circumstances, he would understand why she needed to keep her whereabouts a secret, Laura thought.

'Look I need to take Mia home. My sister Jacky will be there soon. Why don't I meet you somewhere and then we can have a proper talk?

There is a fish restaurant down near the seafront, shall we meet there at 6.00pm. I'll see you there if you would like to?'

Adam breathed a sigh of relief. 'That would be lovely, I can have a walk around for a while and then go and have a coffee somewhere. I was so worried that I would scare you.'

'Right, I'll give Mia her tea and then Jacky can look after her for a couple of hours, I'll see you there then.' She got into her car and reversed out of the car park and sped away.

CHAPTER FIFTEEN

Laura prepared Mia's tea and sat down at the kitchen table with her. Was she doing the right thing agreeing to see Adam, could she trust him?

He did seem genuinely upset. After all, if he had decided to share the money for the plate with her, he would need to know where she lived.

She remembered the morning at the boot fair, he had bought some chips and a soft drink for them both. It was such a little thing but had made quite an impression on her.

She sat waiting for Jacky to come home and she was rather apprehensive what Jacky would say when she told her she was going to meet Adam.

She might think she was being very foolish but there was something about him. He seemed so kind, it was a long time ago that someone had been that kind to her, except for Jacky of course.

Luckily, there were still some men in the world who treated women well, how she wished she had found one.

The kitchen door opened and in came Jacky. 'I just need to sit down. I've been on my feet all day at the salon and my shoes are killing me.' She sat down at the table and kicking off her shoes sat rubbing her feet.

'How was your day serving in the café, did you have many customers? Now the weather is beginning to feel warmer, the town will soon be swarming with holiday makers.'

'Well, I have something to tell you. When I went to pick Mia up at playschool, there was someone waiting for me.' Laura looked rather apprehensive.

'Oh, who was that then, I didn't think you knew many people in the town yet?'

Laura took a deep breath, 'It was Adam Marsh.'

It was Jacky's turn to look shocked. 'How did he find you? Was there anyone with him?'

'No, I asked him if he had brought a reporter with him, but he said no. He had been so upset when he read my letter saying he had put us in danger, that he felt he had to find us to see if we were ok.'

'You didn't tell him where you were living. How did he manage to find you?' Jacky was looking worried.

'He kept going back to the boot-fair every Sunday and last week there was a lady who said Mia went to the same playschool as her daughter, so he decided to come down here today to see if I was waiting for Mia.' Laura was unsure what Jacky would say when she told her that she had agreed to meet him.

'He has taken the plate to an Auction House in London and has left it there as they are having a sale of Chinese Ceramics soon. He thought it would be safer there than in his house.

He is determined to give me half the money when it is sold and of course I will split it with you.

Anyway, he asked if we could meet to talk and I said yes, so we are going to see each other at 6.00pm at the Fish Restaurant.' Laura took a deep breath and sat looking at Jacky waiting for her reaction.

Jacky sat in silence for a few seconds then said, 'Are you sure that is a good idea, he still could be working with the reporter for a good story?'

'I'm sure he is telling the truth, there is just something about him, I don't think he could tell a lie if he tried.

Why would he go to so much trouble to find me, most

people would just have pocketed the money without a thought to the person who sold it to them?'

'I suppose you're right, but you haven't given him this address, have you?'

'No, that's why I said I would meet him at the Restaurant. I won't stay long but I feel I should give him the benefit of the doubt, after all he has gone to a lot of trouble to track me down.' Laura was already wondering if she had done the right thing.

'Don't forget if he can find you, someone else might be able to do the same.' Jacky immediately realized she had said the wrong thing.

'I'm sorry Laura, I didn't mean to scare you, I just worry about you.'

'Don't worry, I think about that every day, it's something I will probably have to live with for the rest of my life.

Always looking over my shoulder wondering if he will ever catch up with me, but there is nothing I can do about it, I just have to hope it never happens.'

Jacky rose from her chair and gave Laura a hug 'Go and put something nice on to meet your knight in shining armour.' She joked.

'I've given Mia her tea. Would you see she goes to bed

at 8pm? I'll try not to be very late.

I was just about to have a wash and change into a dress. I've been serving fish and chips all afternoon and I smell of chip fat.' Laura smiled and realized she was looking forward to seeing Adam again.

Jacky hugged her. 'It's nice to see you smiling for a change. Hurry up and wash your hair and I will style it for you.

I'm looking forward to meeting Mr. Adam Marsh one of these days, anyone who can make you smile, is good guy as far as I'm concerned.'

CHAPTER SIXTEEN

Maxwell sat at his desk looking at his laptop. Where to begin the search for Laura? She did not have any money. He had made sure of that. So therefore, someone must have helped her to escape?

'Was it a man?' Maxwell's face contorted in rage. 'If so, how did she meet him?'

He had put a tracker on her car so that he knew exactly where she went. She must have guessed he had been trailing her, that was why she had left her car behind.

Tracy at the Estate Agents had been no help. Was she lying when she said she did not know where Laura's sister Jacky worked?

There were hundreds of Hair Salons in the City, there was no way he could visit them all. He sat thinking what he could do next.

Laura's Mother and Father were both deceased but perhaps Laura had some close relatives that she had never spoken about?

Maxwell had made sure she had no contact with her friends but maybe she did have some family member who could have helped her?

Maxwell knew Laura's maiden name was Simmons. Her Father was called Alfred and her Mother Kathleen. Perhaps they had brothers or sisters.

Laura could have Aunts and Uncles who were still alive, maybe she had contacted them and asked for help?

Maxwell sat pondering whether he should employ a Private Detective to look for Laura or maybe one of those firms who tracked down the people's relatives so they could build their family tree.

If he could find an aunt or uncle, he could tell them that one of their relatives had died, and that someone might be in line to inherit a large amount of money.

'People would tell you anything if they thought cash was involved.' He sneered.

If one of Laura's relatives could be found, he could visit them. Maybe that was where Laura and Mia were hiding.

Maxwell smiled and thought he would have to look online to see if he could find a firm that dealt with this kind of service.

'I don't care what it costs, money is no object to me. I will be seeing you soon Laura, make no mistake.

When I do find you, you will wish you had never been born. Think you can outwit me?'

Maxwell decided to search the internet in the morning and went to bed with a satisfied smile on his face.

CHAPTER SEVENTEEN

Laura found Adam waiting outside the restaurant. 'I hope you haven't been here for too long?' She said smiling.

'I'm so glad you agreed to meet me. I've already booked a table for two as I thought it might get rather busy.' Adam gazed at Laura he had forgotten what she looked like.

'Thank you, I can't remember the last time I went out for dinner.'

'Well, shall we go in, we can have a drink before we order our meal?' Adam stood back and followed Laura into the Restaurant.

The waiter led them to their table upstairs near a window that looked out at the sea. It was still sunny, the light glistened on the waves as they rippled up the beach.

'Would you like to order some drinks before you have

your dinner?' The waiter stood expectantly.

'Laura, what would you like to drink?' Adam sat looking at her. She was wearing a pretty summer dress which showed off her suntan. Somehow, she looked younger than he remembered, it was so sad that her life had been so dreadful that she had to run away.

'I'll just have a fruit juice, an apple would be fine, but no ice, thank you.'

'Are you sure you wouldn't like some wine?' Adam asked.

'No thank you Adam, I am not much of a drinker, apple juice will be fine, and I shall have to drive home. Wine goes straight to my head.' She laughed.

'What would you like to drink sir?' the waiter asked.

'Could I please have a lager, I'm driving as well, so that will be fine. I'm feeling rather thirsty.'

The waiter handed them the menus, then disappeared to fetch their drinks.

Laura sat studying the menu, she was feeling rather nervous, wondering if she was doing the right thing by accepting Adam's invitation.

Adam could sense she was nervous. He decided to reassure her that he had no intention of revealing her whereabouts.

'I might be able to sleep at night now that I know you and Mia are safe. When I read your letter, I felt physically sick, wondering what I had done?'

Laura looked up from the menu. 'I'm so sorry but I thought that the newspaper might find me. If I tell you my story, you will have to promise me you won't tell anyone where I am?'

'Of course not, I just want to help you if I can.' Adam wondered what she was about to tell him.

The waiter appeared with their drinks. 'Have you decided yet what you would like to eat?'

'What would you like Laura. I think I will have the seafood platter. I remember I had that years ago in this same restaurant.'

Laura said, 'I'll have the fillet of Salmon and new potatoes thank you.'

The waiter wrote down their choices and hurried away.

'Well here goes. I have run away from my husband. He never actually hit me, but I felt like a prisoner in my own home. I was not allowed to have any friends.

He kept track of my every move. I had no money of my own as he didn't want me to work. He just gave me cash for food, and I had to keep all the receipts to show him what I had spent.

I nearly left him soon after we were married but then I became pregnant with Mia, and I had nowhere to run away to.

I am now living in my Auntie Mabel's bungalow. She sadly died a while ago, and as she had no children of her own, she left the bungalow to me and my sister.

Auntie Mabel also left us some money. We were able to get Probate about a month ago and we have decided to use some of the money to refurbish the bungalow. It needs a new kitchen, and the bathrooms need refitting. We think it will be easier to sell once it is brought up to date.

My sister Jacky sent me a letter to tell me my aunt had died, and that is when I was able to make my escape, I finally had somewhere to go. Sadly, I couldn't come to her funeral.

Laura let out a sigh of relief, she had finally told someone what she had been through.

'I don't blame you for leaving him. I find it hard to believe in this day and age, there are still men who think their wives are their property. What era does he think we live in?' Adam shook his head in disbelief.

'The last straw was I found out he had been lying to me. I knew he bought horrible rundown houses, but he told me he refurbished them to a high standard.

I never saw the houses when they were finished, he always said there was a queue of people wanting to move in.

One day a lady and her son knocked on my door. Her little boy looked so ill. She told me her house was riddled with damp and had no central heating. They were both so cold that I asked them to come in and have a hot drink. I was ready to go and see for myself what state the house was in.

My husband suddenly arrived home and screamed at them to get out. I knew then that I had to get away.' Laura looked as if she going to burst into tears.

Adam stretched out across the table and took her hand in his.

'Please don't cry. How did you put up with that man? Was there no one that could have helped you?' Listening to Laura's story had made Adam very angry.

'No, my father died when I was young and sadly my mother died just before I got married. Maxwell, my husband, was so different when we first started to date each other.

He was the perfect gentleman, so kind and affectionate. It was only after we were married that I found out exactly what he was like, but by then, it was too late.'

'Here's the waiter with our food. We won't talk about it

anymore, let us just enjoy our meal.'

Adam smiled at her and said 'After we have had our dinner, we will go for a walk in the fresh air and then we can discuss how we can make sure you never have to go back to him. I want to help you Laura and I want you to trust me.'

Adam was glad he had finally been able to find her. Perhaps he could help, some of the money from the plate might come in useful to set up a new life for her?

'I do trust you Adam, it's just that it's been difficult to trust anyone for years. I hope that we can be friends. This meal looks delicious, let us just enjoy ourselves.'

CHAPTER EIGHTEEN

'It looks as if we will have a lovely sunset.' Adam took Laura by the hand as they walked along the beach. He was so happy he had found her, but would he be able to help her?

'Are you warm enough. You can wear my jacket if you're feeling cold?'

'No, I'm fine You've heard my story, but you haven't told me anything about yourself?'

Laura felt so at ease with Adam, it was if she had known him for years.

'There's not much to tell, I work in an office, but my real passion is for antiques.' Adam laughed.

'That is why I was at the boot fair that day, I was always looking for the one antique that would enable me to leave work and set up my own business.

Your plate was the most valuable piece of China I had ever found. I've still got to go to work though unfortunately.' He laughed.

'Jacky, that's my sister and I are still clearing out my aunt's bungalow. Bless her, Auntie Mabel would never throw anything away.

Uncle Fred was in the Navy and brought loads of presents for her from his travels.' Laura stopped walking and turned to Adam.

'If I tell you where I live maybe you could come and look at some of the pieces that we're not sure what to do with.

Perhaps if they are worth something, we could sell them rather than give them to charity?'

'I would love to help you, after all the plate was a surprise to me. I thought it might be worth a few pounds, but I never dreamed it would be so rare.

I wonder where your Uncle Fred got it from?' Adam stopped and stood looking at Laura, why anyone would want to hurt her, he found it difficult to believe.

'I'll have to ask my sister Jacky if it would be ok for you to come and see us. She was the one who made it possible for me to run away and of course she is very protective of me.

Why don't you give me your phone number and I will have a talk to her, then I will let you know if she thinks it is a good idea?

Actually, I think I should be heading home otherwise she will be worrying about me.' Laura smiled.

'Right, I'll see you back to your car and I will give you my mobile phone number. You can ring me anytime and let me know if I can help. You know, I do want to help you, Laura.'

They walked back to her car and Laura gave him a piece of paper to write on. 'Thank you, it was a lovely evening, I really enjoyed myself.'

'I didn't know how today was going to turn out, I had got so stressed just thinking how I would approach you but I'm glad I decided to come.

I have been so worried about you and Mia.' Adam smiled 'Hopefully, I will be seeing you again, in the not-too distant future?'

'Goodnight, Adam thank you for the lovely dinner.' As Laura drove back to the bungalow, she wondered what Jacky would say, when she arrived home.

CHAPTER NINTEEN

The doorbell rang, Maxwell stood up from his desk and made his way to the front door and opened it.

'Mr. Maxwell Hudson? I am from the firm of Albright and Foster. You sent an e-mail yesterday to the office saying you were interested in researching your wife's family tree?'

'Oh yes, of course, do come in. My wife and daughter are out for the day. I want this to be a surprise for her.

She doesn't know very much about her family, and I thought this would make a lovely present for her.'

'That sounds like a wonderful idea. My name is Mr. Thomson and I have worked for the firm Albright and Foster for many years, and I am sure I will be able to help you.'

'Well don't stand there on the doorstep, let us go into my office and make ourselves comfortable.' Maxwell smiled and led the way along the corridor.

'Can I get you anything to drink? I expect you have had a long drive to get here?'

'Not that far, my firm uses several of my colleagues to visit customers. We cover most of the country. We have found in the past, that families often stay in the vicinity where they were born.

I would appreciate a cup of tea or coffee if that is not too much trouble? Thank you very much.

As I said my name is Alan Thomson and I will be working on your wife's family tree. It is much easier for one person to do the research.'

Mr. Thomson took off his coat and hung it on the back of his chair. He undid his briefcase and brought out a file and placed it on the desk in front of him.

'I'll just be a moment. I've got a pot of coffee on in the kitchen.' Maxwell hurried away to fetch a coffee cup, his mind was whirling on how he would explain what he knew, without raising any suspicion that he was just trying to trace his wife.

'Right here we are, I wasn't sure whether you took sugar, so I have put a sachet in your saucer.' Maxwell smiled as he sat down opposite Mr. Thomson.

'Thank you very much. Well, shall we make a start. Your wife's name is?'

'Laura, her Maiden name was Simmons. We have been married for four and a half years and have a beautiful daughter named Mia, she is three and a half.

She is my little princess, here is a picture of her that I keep on my desk, it was taken for her third birthday, we shall have to have another one taken for her fourth.' Maxwell handed him the picture and sat smiling.

'What a beautiful little girl, does she take after her mother, she has such lovely blond curls?'

'Yes, as you can see my hair is jet black.' Maxwell placed the photograph back on his desk.

'Has Laura got any siblings, a brother or a sister?' Mr. Thomson had begun to write in his file.

'Yes, she has a sister called Jacky, but they seem to have lost touch with each other over the last few years.' Maxwell was finding it hard to keep smiling but did his best to sound positive.

'Do you know if Jacky is married?'

'Not that I know of, so maybe her surname is still Simmons.' Maxwell was clenching his fists underneath the table, till his knuckles turned white.

'Now what about Laura's parents? Are they still alive?' asked Mr. Thomson.

'Sadly, no. Her father was much older than her mother, by 24 years actually, he died when Laura was young, so she hardly knew him.

Her mother died a short while before we were married. It was a sad time for Laura, a girl wants her mother to see her as a bride, doesn't she?'

'Have you got any of the death certificates that I can have, I will copy them and let you have them back.

Also, I would like your wedding certificate and Mia's birth certificate.

How far back in time are you interested in going?' Mr. Thomson sat waiting for an answer.

Maxwell sat thinking for a while. 'Well, I think Laura would like to know if she has any aunts and uncles who are still alive and maybe there are some cousins?'

'If you would like to go and find the certificates that will be of use to me, I will get started on the searches straight away. I am sure I shall be able to find some relatives that your wife may not know she has.

What a very thoughtful present for her. I am sure she will be delighted. Hopefully, it will not take me too long,

I shall be looking at the Census for the era that Laura's

parents were alive. They should tell me the addresses where her parents were living and how many people were residing in the house at the time.'

Maxwell pulled out a file from the draw of his desk. 'I thought you would want these certificates, so I took some time to find them for you. I think there is everything you will need to get you started.'

Mr. Thomson took the file from Maxwell and made his way to the front door.'

'Thank you very much Mr. Thomson, I look forward to hearing from you.

Please do not worry about any expenses, it will be worth it just to see the expression on my wife's face when she sees what I have done for her.' Maxwell smiled to himself.

Maxwell watched as Mr. Thomson drove away, then strode back to his office.

'Yes Laura, just you wait till I catch up with you. I will you know, and hopefully it won't be much longer before I do?'

CHAPTER TWENTY

Laura arrived back at the bungalow and sat waiting for a few minutes. She had really enjoyed herself tonight and Adam seemed such a lovely person. He had been so upset, when she told him the reason why she had fled to this seaside town.

She had already decided that he was an honest young man when he had advertised in the paper that he wanted to share the money for the plate with her.

She was rather anxious what Jacky would say when she told her how the evening had gone and that she had given Adam her telephone number. She could not stop thinking that she might not approve.

'Oh well, I had better go in and face the music.' She got out of the car and locked it and opened the front door.

Jacky was in the sitting room watching the television.

'How did the date go then?' Jacky smiled and beckoned Laura to come and sit on the sofa beside her.

'It wasn't a date. It was just to meet up properly with him. He had given me quite a shock when I saw him in the carpark,

I need not have worried because he is such a nice person. I think I already knew that, but it was lovely to be able to have a proper talk with him.

I told him why I had moved here, and he was genuinely upset when he heard how I had been living with that monster.

We have exchanged telephone numbers and he asked, if there was anything, he could do to help me. I told him we were clearing the bungalow of Auntie Mabel's possessions.' Laura was rather worried what Jacky would have to say.

'Well, if you think he is a very decent person and wanted to help, then I am sure you did the right thing.

If you want him to visit, then I will not have any objection. It is nice to see you looking so happy. I would like to meet him myself. I can usually tell a person's nature as soon as I see them.' Jacky gave Laura a hug.

'I worked out the other day how many miles you came by train from your home to here and it's Two Hundred and

Fifty miles.

Maxwell knows nothing about of your family except you have a sister. I moved down here two years ago so he will not know my address.

I think you will be quite safe. Remember, we looked in the telephone book and picked out the surname Woodman, for you to use when you went for an interview for a job, so he doesn't know the name you go by.

One day, when you get your divorce, you will be able to change it back to Simmons, if you decide that is what you want?' Jacky tried to reassure her.

'I know you're right, but I still keep thinking, that one day he will find me. He is such a horrible devious man. It's going to take me some time before I can really relax.' Laura sighed.

'How was Mia, did she go to bed without too much trouble. Did you have to bribe her with her favourite biscuits?' Laura decided to change the subject.

She had such a lovely time this evening with Adam, that she did not want to spoil it thinking about Maxwell.

'She was fine, we watched some television. She was rather tired and went off to sleep with no trouble, with Bunny of course.'

'Thank You Jacky, you would have made a wonderful

mother. Did you never want to have children?'

'Yes, I would have liked to have had a baby, but I never found the right person. I'm quite happy to be an Auntie, I have all the fun and none of the responsibility' she said laughing.

'Well, I'm tired out now, so I think I'll go to bed' Laura yawned.

'Sweet dreams, Laura. Adam Marsh wouldn't be in any of them, would he?' Jacky laughed.

'Maybe he will, maybe he won't, good night sister dear.' Laura smiled as she made her way to her bedroom.

CHAPTER TWENTY-ONE

'Do come in Mr. Thomson, I hope you have some good news for me.

Laura is out, she has taken Mia to playschool and then she is having her hair done, so she won't be coming home for some time.' Maxwell showed him into his study.

'I have managed to make good progress with this case. As I think I told you, families do tend to stay in the same area where they are born but of course there is always the exception to the rule.' Mr. Thomson smiled.

'Yes, that is extremely interesting, but I can't wait to hear what you have managed to find out.' Maxwell felt like shaking the poor man but instead he gritted his teeth into a fake smile.

'Of course, sir. You must be very excited?' Mr.

Thomson opened his briefcase and took out a file. 'Here you are, I have printed out a copy for you. Let us go through it together?'

Maxwell had to restrain himself from grabbing it out of the poor man's hand.

'To begin, Laura's Grandparents were John and Mary Simmons. Mary's maiden name was Atwood. They had three children, Alfred, Fredrick, and Rose.

Alfred was Laura's father, and he married a Kathleen Harrison and they had two daughters,

Jacky and Laura. As far as I can find out, Jacky has never married.

Laura, of course married you and you have one daughter Mia.

Now Alfred's brother Frederick married a Mabel Whitecroft, but they did not have any children. I have found Frederick's death certificate but so far, I have not found Mabel's.

Alfred's sister Rose remained a Spinster all her life so there are no children from that line.'

Maxwell was trying to conceal his frustration, so far, this stupid little man had not given him any information that might lead to Laura's whereabouts. He smiled politely and nodded his head.

'Well done, but I think it would be nice for Laura if you had found a living relative that we could get in touch with. That would mean that Laura might have uncles, aunts and maybe cousins?'

'Well Sir, if you look down the page you will see that Laura's Mother's maiden name was Harrison and she had a sister called Elizabeth. She married a man called Andrew Mortimer and they had one son called Charles. Charles is still living, so he is Laura's cousin.'

Maxwell took a deep breath, 'At last I have a name, he could be sheltering Laura?' He said to himself.

'Do you have an address for Charles, it would be lovely to contact him and see whether he would like to come here and meet Laura. That would be a lovely surprise for her.

She has never spoken of a Cousin Charles, so maybe, she does not know of his existence?

When I show her the completed Family Tree, he could be waiting in another room ready to make an entrance.' Maxwell smiled.

Maxwell was really thinking 'I'll find him first and if he is hiding Laura, he had better watch out?'

Maxwell looked at Mr. Thomson and said 'You have done a wonderful job, thank you so much.

I will have Laura's Family Tree printed on parchment

and have it embellished with a family crest that I have ordered to be created.'

'You will want all the death certificates and Birth certificates that I have managed to obtain. I have them here in my briefcase, I am sure your wife would enjoy looking through them?'

Mr. Thomson thought Maxwell was in a hurry to be rid of him.

'Of course, she would. Have you got your bill? I will write you a cheque straight away.'

Maxwell was in a hurry to look for Mr. Charles Mortimer.

'Here you are Sir, you will see I have listed all the documents I have found and of course the time I have spent on the investigations.'

'Thank you so much. Cheap at the price, Laura will be so happy with her surprise present. I can hardly wait for it to be printed. We shall have a party to celebrate.'

Maxwell quickly wrote the cheque and handed it to Mr. Thomson. 'I will be recommending your firm to all of my friends. You have done such a wonderful job.'

Maxwell stood while Mr. Thomson examined his cheque then shook his hand and led the way to the front door.

Mr. Thomson said 'Well goodbye Sir, I am so glad I

have been able to help. I am sure your wife will be delighted with her present.' He said smiling.

'Oh, she will be over the moon when she sees what I have managed to find out, truly you have made my day.'

Maxwell came back to his office. He could not stop smiling, 'Well Mr. Charles Mortimer, here I come, you'll wish you had never been born.'

CHAPTER TWENTY-TWO

Adam could not stop smiling as he got out of bed the morning after he had taken Laura to dinner.

He was now able to relax. He had been so worried about her and her little girl for weeks. Finding out that they were both safe and had somewhere to live was wonderful news.

The Auction house had e-mailed to tell him when the plate was going to be in the sale of Chinese Ceramics and had put an asking price of £32, 000 pounds online and there would also be several telephone bidders from around the world.

Hopefully, he would soon be able to give Laura her share of the money and perhaps it would be of help to her situation.

He had made his mind up that he would ring her later this afternoon and see if he could come for a visit at the weekend?

As for the reason she had escaped from her husband, Adam found it hard to believe that in this day and age someone could be so cruel as to make his wife feel like a prisoner in her own home.

He thought that her husband must be an extremely sick individual if he needed to make Laura's life such a misery. The problem was that he was still out there somewhere, and Laura must be constantly wondering if he would turn up on her doorstep one day.

Adam sighed, what could he do apart from trying to make her feel more secure? He could try to bring some joy into her life, but as he was working, he could only see her at weekends.

He thought that finding her would give him peace of mind but in-fact now he knew her situation, he was more worried than before.

Well, there was nothing he could do about it this morning, so he quickly washed and dressed for work and tried not to think about the monster who had made Laura's life such a misery.

The day could not go fast enough, Adam was glad when

the afternoon was over. He went and sat in his car and dialed Laura's number.

'Hello' Laura answered.

'Laura, it's Adam, I hope you are ok? Thank you for coming out to see me last night. It was nice to finally meet. I was wondering if I could come down on Saturday then I could look at your Aunt Mabel's collections?'

'That would be lovely Adam. We could do some work and then if the weather is fine, we could take Mia down to the beach. My Saturdays are free, so we could take a picnic for lunch.

I want you to meet my sister Jacky, she has been so kind to me. I could never have come all this way if there had been nowhere for Mia and me to stay. I think you will like her.

She is a hairdresser, so she is always busy on Saturdays. Perhaps we could all go out in the evening for a meal?'

'That sounds like a good idea, I will be looking forward to it.

Please take care of yourself. The plate is going be auctioned soon. It will be good to have it sold. It was a worry when I had it at home. Hopefully, it will reach the auction price.' Adam said.

'Of course, I will share half the money with Jacky, she

deserves to buy something for herself.

I don't know what I would have done if Jacky hadn't been there for me.

I look forward to seeing you on Saturday, take care of yourself.' Laura smiled to herself as she put the telephone down.

Adam sat for a few moments in the car. Life was strange, he had only seen Laura twice, once at the boot fair and then last night.

He felt as if he had known her all his life. Maybe buying the plate was written in the stars. Saturday could not come soon enough.

CHAPTER TWENTY-THREE

Maxwell had found the address of Mr. Charles Mortimer. His family had lived in the same house for years.

It did not take him long to drive there. The house was on a leafy avenue and was a substantial building. The Mortimer family were obviously well off as the house was set back from the road and had a paved drive up to the front door.

A large box hedge curved around the drive and there were window boxes full of brightly coloured flowers.

Maxwell got out of the car and locked it. He stood for a few minutes, going over in his mind, how to approach this man.

He would try to be calm so as not to antagonize him but somehow, he would need to get inside the house.

Maxwell walked slowly up the drive, past an expensive car that was parked near the front door. Obviously, Mr. Mortimer was a man of substance, Maxwell took a deep breath and rang the bell.

It was a few moments before the door was opened by a portly gentleman with silver grey hair.

'Mr. Charles Mortimer?'

'Yes, what can I do for you?' the gentleman looked puzzled.

'My name is Maxwell Hudson. Does that mean anything to you?'

'No, I don't think so, we haven't met before, have we?'

'I think, you know my wife Laura, she is your cousin?' Maxwell was staring at him, trying to keep his temper under control.

'I'm sorry but I have never heard of a Laura, you must be mistaken. I do not have any family, sadly my mother and father are no longer with us.

I suppose, they might have known your wife, but unfortunately, I never have. What is this all about anyway?'

'Your mother was called Elizabeth and she had a sister called Kathleen. Laura is Kathleen's daughter so therefore she is your cousin.'

'Well, that's all very interesting, but as I say, I don't

know your wife. If you do not mind, I am rather busy.' Charles began to shut the door.

Maxwell was too fast for him. He stuck his foot in the gap and pushed the door open.

'What do you think you are doing? Get out of my house or I will call the police. Are you mad?'

Charles stood back and pulled out his mobile phone and dialed 999. Maxwell grabbed it from his hand.

Maxwell pushed past him and started to rush around the ground floor calling out 'Laura, you had better get yourself down here, you don't want me to hurt your cousin, do you?'

He raced up the stairs and started looking into all the bedrooms. There was no sign of Laura or Mia anywhere.

'I can assure you I am not interested in your wife, I live here with my husband Patrick, we were married a few months ago.

You have obviously got the wrong person. If your wife has run away with a man, it is certainly not me. Now get out of my house before the police arrive!' Charles was looking terrified.

Maxwell had to admit that it seemed unlikely that Laura was living here, and he pushed Charles out of the way and strode back to his car and drove off at speed down the road.

He drove for a few miles and then parked up near a public house. He sat shaking with fury. Where was she? he really thought he had found her.

Someone, must be hiding her? He would have to start all over again trying to figure out where she had gone.

He decided to go into the public house and have a stiff drink. 'Find you I will Laura, even if it takes the rest of my life.'

CHAPTER TWENTY-FOUR

Adam was looking forward to seeing Laura, Saturday could not come fast enough.

Laura said they could go for a picnic after they had worked on the collections of her Auntie Mabel, so he had bought a few treats to take with him.

He had also bought a toy for Mia. He had looked around the toy shop for something for a young girl but had asked the shop assistant for some help.

She advised him that unicorns were very popular at the moment, so he settled on a fluffy white one.

He was up early on Saturday morning, eager to set off for his meeting with Laura. He packed the food he had bought for their picnic and Mia's toy.

Luckily, it was a bright sunny day, so the beach would be

a pleasant place to eat.

He set off for the drive down to the coast. The roads were fairly busy, a day at the seaside was obviously appealing on such a lovely day.

After about an hour, he reached the bungalow and pulled up outside. He got out and stood looking at the view across the sand. The sea was a long way out and Adam smiled to himself. He had not felt this happy for some time.

He was not sure why he was feeling this way, when the front door opened. Laura was standing there with Mia by her side waving to him.

'Hello Adam. You're nice and early. Mia is excited to see you. Come on in and have a cup of coffee before we start work.' Laura smiled.

Adam followed her indoors and they went into the kitchen.

'I've brought a few things for the picnic, perhaps we had better put them in the fridge for now.' Adam started to unpack the bags he had brought in from the car.

'Oh, that's so kind of you. Mia, look what Adam has brought, some of your favourite goodies.'

'I hoped you would like sausage rolls and scotch eggs. It's not really a picnic without them.'

Adam smiled at Mia. 'I don't suppose you remember

me, do you? I bought that big plate from your mummy when you were at the boot fair.'

'I think I do? Mummy says you bought us some chips from the Burger Van, and I can remember eating those.'

'Laura, I have bought Mia a little present, but I thought I had better ask you if I can give it to her.' Adam whispered.

'Of course, you can. Mia, Adam has brought something for you. Isn't it exciting, I wonder what it can be?' Laura beckoned to Mia. Adam was holding a rather large bag from a well-known toy shop.

'Here you are, the lady in the shop said little girls like these animals. What are you going to call her?'

Mia took the bag and proceeded to pull out the unicorn. Mia's eyes shone and she turned to Adam and said 'I love her. I'm going to show her to Bunny, and they can be best friends. I'm not sure what to call her, can you think of something Mummy?'

'I never had a unicorn when I was a little girl. They are magical animals which fairies play with. Perhaps Adam can think of a name?' Laura looked across at Adam and smiled.

'I think that this unicorn is a little girl, so she should have a pretty name. Unicorns can fly through the air, so does blossom on the trees when it is windy. Blossom would be a lovely name. It starts with B and so does Bunny.'

Adam laughed.

'I love that name. I am going to show her to Bunny right now.'

'Aren't you going to say thank you to Adam first.' Laura smiled and winked at Adam.

'Thank you very much Adam, I love her.' With that Mia disappeared into the bedroom.

'Thank goodness for that, I hadn't got a clue what to buy a little girl, but she seems to be pleased with it.' Adam sighed.

'It was so kind of you, she had to leave lots of her old toys when we ran away. I have bought her a few things but the bedroom she had at home was fit for a princess.' Laura looked sad.

'A beautiful bedroom is not necessary to show how much you love her. I am sure as she got older, the same thing would have happened to Mia. Her father would have wanted to control her life, just like he did yours.'

'You're quite right, I know I did the right thing but there are times when I wonder if I will be able to give her the life she deserves?'

'Mia seems happy enough to me. Come on, let's get on with some work. It is such a lovely day to be stuck indoors. The sooner we get on with sorting the things you might like to sell, the sooner we can have our picnic on the beach. I expect Mia loves making sandcastles.'

Laura made Adam a cup of coffee, then led him into the dining room.

'Wow, I wasn't expecting this in an old lady's bungalow.' He stood staring at the spears, shields and masks which were dotted around the walls and some of them looked rather scary.

Laura laughed. 'Jacky and I didn't like to come in here at night, it was too frightening. They didn't seem quite so scary during the day. Perhaps we thought they came to life once it was dark.'

Adam walked around peering at them. 'I think some of them would make quite a lot of money. There are people who collect this type of art.

They would be carved by hand in the villages.' He stood scrutinizing one in particular which was very ornate.

'I'll take a few photographs on my mobile phone, there might be some for sale on the Internet.

I think there are some similar carvings in one of my antique books. It would be best if the whole collection went to a specialist sale.'

'My uncle Fred brought them home from his journeys around the world. He was in the Merchant Navy. I am not sure that Auntie Mabel was very keen on them, but she would never have told Uncle Fred that. They loved each other so much.' Laura sighed.

Adam went around the room taking photographs of the tribal art and when he had finished, he said 'Shall I help you take them down, I think it would be quite difficult for you to do it on your own. Have you any cardboard boxes we could pack them in?'

'Yes, I have been collecting them from the local supermarket, they said I could have them. I've been storing them in Uncle Fred's shed in the garden.'

'Let me come with you, they will be difficult to carry on your own.' Laura led him to the shed, and they came back to the house with several large boxes.

'Right, I'll try to lever them off the wall and then hand them to you. They have obviously been up here for years so they might be stuck.'

Adam started at one end of the room and Laura wrapped the masks and shields in newspaper and stowed them away in the boxes.

It took a long time to remove them all from the walls. 'We can see what the wallpaper used to be like, very floral and bright.'

'The room looks strange now that they are all gone but

it had to be done. We need to get on with stripping the wallpaper off and putting some paint on the walls.'

Laura looked at Adam and smiled. He didn't seem to mind that he was spending his Saturday off, working on the bungalow.

'Well, I think we have earned our picnic on the beach, the sun is shining, and the fresh air will do us good.'

'I'll get Mia ready and start putting the nice things you brought for us in a cool box. Would you like to wash your hands in the bathroom, all the tribal art was very dusty? It's on the right as you come in the front door.'

Laura went to find Mia who was watching the television with Bunny and Blossom sitting on the sofa beside her.

Adam came back from the bathroom and looked around the living room.

'Laura, I have seen something on the mantlepiece, has this been here for long?' Adam asked.

'Oh, that's the white rabbit. We were not allowed to touch that when we were little. Auntie Mabel would sometimes take it down and wind it up for us. The rabbit pops out of the cabbage leaves and looks as if he is eating it, then pops down again. Do you think it is worth something?' Laura handed it down to Adam.

'It's called an Automaton. It should play music. It was

made by the company called Roullet and Decamps, circa 1890. I saw one for sale not long ago on the Internet. It sold for £1,320.'

'How do you know all about these antiques? Did you study them at college?' Laura asked.

'No, my mother and father used to take me to Antique fairs when I was a young boy.

My mother had me rather late in life, I think I was a surprise baby, so I grew up going to National Trust Estates and places of interest like Museums and Art Galleries.

It was just second nature for me to be interested in China and paintings. I was rather a shy child. I did not have very much in common with the other pupils in my class.

Another of my parent's hobbies was going to the Theatre. I still love to go. Have you ever been to the Theatre?' Adam smiled.

'No, I haven't but I would have liked to.' Laura said.

'Maybe we could go sometime in the future? That is if you don't think I will bore you to tears?' Adam laughed.

'I don't find you boring at all. It's nice to talk to someone who has something interesting to say. Maxwell was not one for much conversation at all, except to criticize me.' Laura sighed.

'Don't let us talk about him anymore. What is going to

happen to the bungalow when you have finished clearing away all of your Aunt Mabel's things?'

'Jacky and I are going to try and bring it up to the 21st century. It needs so much work. A new kitchen, bathroom, and general decoration. Then we hope to sell it and each of us will have enough hopefully to buy ourselves a flat or something.

I will be sorry to see it sold, we had some lovely holidays here with our Auntie and Uncle.'

'I can see why you love it here, which reminds me, we are supposed to be going to the beach. The sun is shining, the tide is up just in time for some paddling.'

'You're quite right Adam. Mia Darling, we are going to the beach. Get your bucket and spade.'

CHAPTER TWENTY-FIVE

Adam was happy to go down to the bungalow every weekend. When the decision to sell some of the items in Aunt Mabel's collections had been made, he then offered to help with the decoration and refurbishment of the bungalow.

He had been introduced to Jacky that first Saturday and she was happy to see how Laura and Adam were with each other. Adam was ready to help with anything that needed doing, painting, stripping wallpaper and carpentry jobs around the bungalow.

She thought it was lovely to see Laura laughing and smiling. Mia too, seemed to have bonded with Adam. He would play with her in the garden and carry her on his shoulders when they went for a long walk along the beach.

Jacky wished that Laura had met Adam before she had married Maxwell but sadly life was not always that simple. There was still the danger that Maxwell would suddenly appear one day, and Jacky was not sure what would happen if he did.

The day of the London auction of the plate arrived and much to Adam's delight it went for the asking price of £32,000 pounds. Of course, there were costs to be paid but as soon as the cheque arrived in Adam's bank, he came down to see Laura and presented a cheque to her. She was amazed with the amount of money and immediately shared half with Jacky.

The refurbishment of the bungalow was going well, and Aunt Mabel's will, had been through Probate and the money in the Building Society had been shared between the two sisters.

Everything was turning out just as the sisters had hoped, until one afternoon Laura was sitting watching television when the news came on.

Laura stared in disbelief at the picture on the screen. She called for Jacky to come quickly and see.

'That's Blackwell Road. Maxwell has several houses in that street.' Laura listened intently to the News Reader who was standing in front of the house.

'Yesterday there had been a bad water leak at this building. The Water board sent out workmen to dig up the garden to find the cause of the problem. During the excavation to find the burst pipe, a bundle was found, buried under the patio and on examination was found to contain human remains.

The house had several people living there, they have been taken to the Police Station for questioning.

The police have cordoned off the house and the forensic team are at work there now.

The owner of the house has been contacted and is helping the police with their enquiries.'

Laura sat there in shock. Jacky came and put her arm around her.

Laura shook her head in disbelief. 'The newsreader said there were several people living there. I've been in one of those houses and they are tiny. Just about room for four people.'

'Unfortunately, there are some landlords that turn a blind eye to overcrowding as long as they get plenty of money.

They are sometimes illegal immigrants who can't find anywhere better to live and are fearful that they might be transported.' Jacky looked at Laura who was now obviously upset.

'After how he treated that poor lady with her son who was obviously ill, nothing would surprise me about Maxwell, but a dead body! I wonder who it can be. I suppose the forensic team will have to take it back to a laboratory to find out who it is?' Laura shuddered.

'Well, please don't upset yourself, there is nothing you can do. We shall have to buy a newspaper tomorrow to find out exactly what is happening.

Until then, maybe Maxwell will get some sort of police sentence for allowing illegal immigrants to live in his houses. Serve him right. I always knew he was a horrible human being for the way that he treated you.' Jacky said.

'Adam is coming down on Saturday, he seems clever at finding out information on his laptop. Maybe he can find the full story and then we can learn what is happening.

I suppose there might be more on the news tonight.' Laura always looked forward to seeing Adam but now Saturday could not come fast enough.

Laura had begun to realize that she was becoming very fond of Adam. How could she not? He was so helpful, no job was too much trouble, and he never complained about the work involved.

He was so lovely with Mia, and she obviously enjoyed

his visits. Laura knew until the problem of Maxwell could somehow be settled that nothing could come of Adam and her relationship with him.

If she wanted to divorce Maxwell, he would have to know where she was, and she could not risk that happening anytime soon.

She was not sure how Adam felt about her, but after all, he knew the situation she was in.

Laura sighed and tried not to worry, but that was not easy as the thought of Maxwell arriving one day was never far from her mind.

CHAPTER TWENTY-SIX

Laura had rung Adam and told him the news about Blackwell Road and the body being found in the garden.

Adam had been on his laptop and managed to find out more information on the BBC News Channel.

There were interviews with some of the neighbours in the road. Most of them said they had been worried about the number of people going in and out of the house in question.

There had been a problem with noise and arguments, but when they reported it to the landlord, he seemed totally uninterested.

Maxwell owned several houses in the same road. He was never very helpful when there was a problem, and most of the tenants knew that it was useless asking for work to be done.

Obviously, the thought that someone had been murdered was frightening but none of the neighbours had seen or heard anything suspicious.

The remains had been taken away to be examined by the forensic team in order to find the cause of death and to complete the investigation to identify the victim.

Adam was glad it was Saturday and that he would be able to see Laura who had sounded extremely upset on the phone. She was standing at the front door waiting for him to arrive.

'I'm so glad that you are here Adam. When I saw the road where I had taken Maxwell when I was working at the Estate Agents, it made me feel sick.

I remember the house was in a terrible state, and I had to come out as there was a rat or a mouse which ran across the floor. He assured me that his workmen would soon make the house look like new and of course I believed him.

We shall just have to wait and see if the Police can identify the body. I wonder how long it had been in the garden. Apparently, it was under the patio, that would mean that someone had buried it sometime ago.'

'Try not to worry too much about it. There have been several people living there for months or maybe years, so it could be anyone. I am just worried whether they will want to be in touch with you, as you are Maxwell's wife.'

'I've already thought of that, do you think the police will be able to find me. I feel as if I am a suspect, I had no idea what Maxwell was doing, letting the house out to so many people.

After the way he treated that poor woman and her little boy, nothing would surprise me.'

Laura looked as if she was about to burst into tears.

Adam put his arms around her and gave her a hug. He really wanted to kiss her but thought that this was not the right time to tell her that he was falling in love with her. He just wanted her to know that he would be there for her no matter what the future brought.

'I'll keep looking on the website to try and find out anymore news but let us just forget about it today. You and Mia need some fresh air. You won't do any good sitting indoors and worrying about this, let's go to the beach and take a picnic.

I've already done some shopping and after a week stuck behind a desk, I need to clear my head.'

'I don't know what I would do without you Adam. I try not to let Jacky know that I'm so upset, she has been so kind to Mia and me. She was the one who helped me escape.

You probably don't need to hear all my troubles either, if it all gets too much for you, I'll understand.'

'I'm always going to be here for you Laura. I'm not going anywhere. Come on let's get Mia ready for the beach and try to put this out of your mind for a few hours. The work in the bungalow will have to wait for another day.'

CHAPTER TWENTY-SEVEN

'Mr. Maxwell Hudson?'

'Yes, who are you?'

'My name is Detective Conroy, and this is Detective Blake. We would like to come in and talk to you about your house in Blackwell Road. I believe you are the owner. Have you been watching the news on television this morning?'

'No, I've been in my study all morning. What is this all about? I own several houses in Blackwell Road, has there been a fire or something?'

'Unfortunately, Mr. Hudson, the Water Board had to send workmen to your house to deal with a burst pipe. It was leaking very badly and there has been some flooding.' Detective Conroy stopped talking.

'I don't have anything to do with the upkeep of the

houses, I have builders who see to that side of things for me.' Maxwell wondered where this conversation was heading?

'Please may we come inside Mr. Hudson. We would rather continue with our enquires indoors if you don't mind?'

'Very well, but surely the Water Board is dealing with the problems so I can't see how I can help you.'

The two Detectives stepped inside and carefully took time to wipe their feet on the doormat.

'I hope we haven't trod any mud on your carpet. The garden at no. 24 Blackwell Road is a quagmire. The burst pipe has caused some damage to the brickwork at the back of the house.'

Maxwell led the way to his study. 'Can I get either of you gentlemen a cup of tea or coffee?'

'No thank you, we just need some information about No. 24, then we must get back to the Police Station.' They both sat down facing Maxwell who was sitting behind his desk.

'Would you mind telling us how many people are renting No. 24 Blackwell Road?'

'Well, it is only a two bedroomed terrace house, so if I remember rightly, it's a family of four people, they have been there for several years.'

'That is very strange, the neighbours we have spoken to all said that people were coming and going at all times of the day and night.

Some people would arrive early in the morning as if they had been on a night shift, then other people would shortly set off for work.' Detective Conroy stopped and looked at Maxwell to see if there was any reaction to what he had just told him.

Maxwell stared back at him. 'This is news to me. I will have to evict the family that is living there. They are obviously renting some of the rooms without my permission.

I never collect the rent on the houses, I have someone to do this for me. I will definitely have a word with the rent collector to find out if he knew what was going on.'

'Mr. Hudson, I did have a quick look around No.24, it's in a dreadful state of repair. There is only one bathroom which is in a disgusting state. The bedrooms have piles of mattresses against the walls, which is rather odd don't you think?'

'As I have already told you, I have nothing to do with the daily running of these houses. I will be having an immediate meeting with my builders as soon as you leave.'

Maxwell hoped that the Detectives had finished asking questions, but they seemed in no hurry to leave.

'All the people who appeared to be living in the house have been taken to the Police Station to be questioned and make statements, this obviously will take some time.'

Maxwell seemed rather shocked. 'That seems rather over the top for just a water leak.' He was feeling increasingly uneasy.

'Not really sir, you see when the workmen were digging in the garden to find the burst pipe, they found something very unusual.'

Maxwell's face was giving nothing away.

Detective Conroy continued. 'They found a bundle of old carpet and when they pulled it open it revealed the remains of a dead body.'

'Good God, how dreadful. Of course, those houses are very old and over the years who knows how many people have come and gone. What is going to happen next? Presumably, no one will be able to live there for some time?'

'It is now a crime scene. A through search of the surrounding area will be carried out and then the remains will be handed over to the coroner. The house and garden have been cordoned off.

Photographs have been taken of every detail, even the pattern on the carpet.

Hopefully, they will be able to find out who the unfortunate individual is?'

Detective Conroy sat in silence waiting for some kind of reaction from Maxwell.

'I hope you will find out who the poor soul is. If you will excuse me Detectives, I have several meetings today. Please keep me informed of your progress.' Maxwell rose and stood by the door. He seemed in a hurry to bring the interview to a close.

'Well thank you for your time, Mr. Hudson. I will definitely let you know of any progress we make.

Do you live here on your own, I see there are two cars on the driveway?'

'No, my wife and daughter are away at the moment, on a little holiday, they should be back soon.' Maxwell smiled.

'So, you will be available over the next few weeks if we need to contact you? No holidays planned?' Detective Conroy asked.

'No. I shall be here if you need any more information, but I don't know how I can help you.

I am so shocked at what has happened. I will definitely have to phone my Rent Collector and find out what has been going on.'

Maxwell showed the Detectives to the front door and smiled 'Goodbye, I hope you soon discover the identity of that poor soul.'

Maxwell made his way back to his study, sat down and began to shake. 'Oh my God, they have found her.'

CHAPTER TWENTY-EIGHT

An elderly man made his way to the Reception Desk in the Police Station.

'Good morning sir how can I help you?' asked the officer on duty.

'I would like to see someone in charge of the investigation at 24 Blackwell Road.' The old gentleman was leaning on a stick and looked agitated.

'Have you some information that you would like to discuss with the officers in charge?'

'I think they will be extremely interested in what I have to tell them.'

'Very well sir, I will ring their office and see whether Detective Conroy or Detective Blake are available to see you.' The officer dialed a number.

'Detective Conroy, I have a gentleman in reception who would like to talk to you about 24 Blackwell Road.' He paused and turned to the gentleman waiting, 'What is your name sir?'

'My name is Colin Burton, but I don't think the Detective would know me.'

The officer relayed this to the Detective and listened for a few minutes then said 'Detective Conroy is coming to take you to his office. Would you please sit down, and wait for him?'

Mr. Burton sat down. His hands were shaking. He kept looking at his watch and was breathing rapidly.

Detective Conroy soon arrived, introduced himself and asked Mr. Burton to follow him to his office.

'Please take a seat Mr. Burton. I believe you have some information concerning No.24 Blackwell Road.' The Detective sat behind his desk and waited for Mr. Burton to speak.

'I know Mr. Maxwell Hudson, the owner of the house in question. You see he was married to my daughter.' He stopped and taking out a handkerchief, proceeded to wipe his eyes.

'Do you mind Mr. Burton, if I tape this interview, it might help to have a copy for the future?'

'No, I don't mind if you think it will be of help.' Mr. Burton continued. 'My daughter told me she was very unhappy married to Maxwell. He wanted to control every aspect of her life.

He would not let her see her friends. He didn't want her to work outside the home. He didn't even want her to visit me and my wife.

We hardly ever saw her and when we did, she seemed frightened of him, and she told us she was thinking of leaving him.' Mr. Burton stopped talking, he seemed to be having difficulty breathing.

'I'm extremely sorry to hear that Mr. Burton, but what has this to do with No. 24 Blackwell Road?'

'Not long after her last visit, Mr. Hudson rang and said that Julia (that was my daughter's name) had left him, leaving a letter telling him that she had left the country to go abroad to live with her boyfriend.

He was extremely angry and abusive about our daughter, calling her a slut. He said he would be divorcing her.'

My wife and I were distraught, we had no idea where she had gone. She had never mentioned a boyfriend to us.

We never heard from her again. No letters, no phone calls to let us know where she was and that she was safe.

Julia would never have let her mother worry about her

like that. Julia was our only child. It was heart breaking.

It definitely was the reason my wife became ill and sadly she died four years after Julia went missing…' Mr. Burton stopped talking and sat with his head bowed.

'Are you suggesting Mr. Burton that Mr. Hudson had something to do with the disappearance of your daughter.' Detective Conroy sat while Mr. Burton composed himself.

'That's exactly what I am saying. He divorced my daughter after she had been missing for seven years, which apparently, he could do so according to the law. He wanted to marry his new girlfriend. I pity her if he treats her like he treated my daughter?'

'So, you think that Maxwell Hudson was lying when he told you your daughter had gone abroad?' Detective Conway had begun to write something in his notepad.

'Yes, I do. When I saw on television that human remains had been found at 24 Blackwell Road, I thought that….' Mr. Burton had to stop.

'You think that the human remains might be your daughter?' Detective Conroy looked at the poor man sitting opposite and waited until he was able to continue.

'I want you to take a DNA sample from me and hopefully you can get some DNA evidence from whoever has been buried in that garden?

We did report Julia missing after about two years but were told as she was an adult, they would not be pursuing our request for her to be traced.' Mr. Burton sighed and wiped his eyes again.

'I think that it is a wonderful suggestion for a DNA test and hopefully it will put your mind to rest that it isn't Julia but some other poor soul who has been buried there for years.

I will make the arrangements for you to have the test as soon as possible. I am extremely grateful that you came to see me Mr. Burton. You absolutely did the right thing.

Please would you fill in this form with your name and address and your telephone number. We will be contacting you soon and hopefully, after you have had the DNA test, we will have some good news for you.'

Detective Conroy accompanied Mr. Burton back to reception and wished him well.

He then returned to his office and played back the recording of the interview with Mr. Burton.

'I think it is now time to have Mr. Maxwell Hudson come to the Police Station to answer some questions. I think I will enjoy that immensely.'

CHAPTER TWENTY-NINE

Maxwell sat with his head bowed. 'I should have known that someone would find her one day! I wonder how long it will take for the forensic team to identify her body?'

His mind was racing. 'I need to think what to do. At least most of my money is in offshore accounts. The question is where to go?'

He stood up and opened a cupboard. He took out a large black hold-all then unhooked the picture hanging behind his desk which revealed a wall safe.

He entered the numbers to unlock it and swiftly began to transfer £50. and £20. notes into the holdall until it was full to the brim.

He had always told his Rent Collector to accept only cash, strictly no cheques or credit cards.

Cash was always useful as it could open so many doors.

He suddenly thought 'I nearly left my laptop behind. I wouldn't want anyone to look at what is on it.' He picked it up and laid it on the top of all the cash.

'I will have to find somewhere that has Wi-fi, I'll need to keep a watch out for anything on the news. The police might start looking for me when they find out the identity of the body.'

He sat for a while, wondering what to do next? He peered into the safe to see if it was completely empty when he spied something at the back. He pulled it towards him. It was a faded old passport.

He opened it and sat staring at the photograph, as the memories came flooding back.

Maxwell had run away from home when he was just nineteen years old to start a new life in Britain. His father owned a Taverna and Dimitri Costas, his son, worked as a waiter.

During the summer, Tourists from mainland Greece, would come to the island by ferry for the day and brought plenty of money to spend in the village.

Huge expensive yachts would dock in the harbour, and the wealthy owners would come in the evening to dine at the Taverna and get drunk.

He thought the women from the yachts were vulgar, they wore revealing outfits that left nothing to the imagination. They made him feel embarrassed with their suggestions as to what they wanted him to do. A Greek lady would not behave like that.

They left him large tips and he kept some of them for himself hiding the money in a box under his bed.

Dimitri envied them as they sailed away the next morning, wishing he could go too.

Winter was worst when the tourists stopped coming. Money was short, no big tips for him to save.

His father still had plenty of work for him to do. The house and the Taverna needed repairs.

The family also had some land where they kept a donkey, goats, and chickens. Dimitri was expected to look after the animals.

His father had chosen a girl in the village and said that Dimitri should marry her and give him grandchildren. He had no intention of getting married and never leaving the island.

One night, Dimitri packed a rucksack, left a note for his mother, and disappeared intending to make a new life for himself in Britain.

He managed to get work in restaurants and learnt to

speak English by listening to the radio. He couldn't afford to buy himself somewhere to live in London, so he decided to travel up to the north of England where he had heard that houses were much cheaper.

Over the years he began to buy rundown old properties and soon owned a few so that he could give up work and just live off the rent from the houses.

Maxwell sat thinking, staring at the photograph in his passport. Perhaps it was time to go home. Greece had plenty of small islands where he could hide. Maybe he could buy a small boat and sail wherever he wanted.

His mother and father were probably deceased by now. He sat wondering what had happened to the Taverna and the land?

He made his way upstairs to the bathroom and began to shave off his beard. He stood looking at his reflection.

The young teenager had managed to make a good life for himself since leaving Greece.

It was a pity that his choice of women had been unfortunate, he wondered if he should have taken his father's advice and married a Greek girl, they were brought up to obey their husbands.'

He found another holdall and started to pack, only jeans and tee-shirts. He looked ruefully in his wardrobe at the expensive suits and shirts, knowing that he would have no need for that sort of clothing in the future.

He went back down to his office and picked up the photograph of Mia that he kept on his desk.

He sat down and looked at it. He could not care less whether he saw Laura again, but he loved his daughter. If only he could find her, Mia could come to Greece with him?

'I'll have one last look through all the paperwork that Mr. Thomson brought me, perhaps I have missed something. Maybe there was a clue in one of the certificates.'

He began to read the death certificates, the majority of the people listed, had died many years ago.

He then began to search the marriage certificates, there was one for Fredrick and Mabel Whitecroft. He had found Fredrick's death certificate but not Mabel's.

He decided to look on the Census, it showed an address where they had both lived for years, a Kent seaside town. It had the house number and the road.

'Mabel Whitecroft was Laura's Aunt. Perhaps this is where Laura had taken Mia?'

Maxwell had decided to drive to a Port where he might find a ship that could take him to Greece.

'Why don't I try to find the address listed on the Census first. Who knows, maybe Laura had travelled to Kent to stay with her aunt?'

He quickly went back upstairs and made sure he had everything he needed. He decided to go immediately, it was the middle of the night. Hopefully, no one was watching the house.

He thought he would drive Laura's car. His Mercedes would not allow him to keep a low profile. He turned off all the outside lights and stood composing himself. He opened the back door and crept slowly down the side of the house and unlocked Laura's car.

He put the two holdalls in the boot, then he bent down and removed the tracker that he had installed in the wheel arch and then sat in the driver's seat. He sat still for a few seconds taking deep breaths, trying to compose himself, then he took off the hand brake.

The drive was on a slant leading down to the road and after a while, the car began to roll slowly downwards.

On reaching the bottom, Maxwell started the engine and turned the car in the direction of the motorway. 'Well goodbye Maxwell Hudson, hello again Dimitri Costas.'

CHAPTER THIRTY

Maxwell drove one hundred and fifty miles through the darkness until the sun began to rise. He was totally exhausted. 'I must stop and have a sleep, or I will crash the car.'

He decided to look for a service station where he could have a rest. He soon saw a sign and not long after, he turned off the motorway.

He decided not to park where there could be cameras, so he turned off down a side road and sat closing his eyes. He soon fell asleep and then woke with a start. For a few seconds he could not remember where he was.

He took a few deep breaths and decided to make his way to the restaurant to have something to eat and drink.

As he walked through the carpark, he realized that there

were lorries that had been parked for the night and the idea came to him that maybe he could hitch a ride with someone who was on the way down to the coast?

He entered the restaurant and made his way to the queue for breakfast. He thought 'Perhaps I should have a cooked meal, who knows when I will be able to eat again?'

He paid for his meal and carried his tray over to a table. He was sitting near enough to hear some of the lorry drivers discussing where they were going and how far they had already driven.

Some had spent the night in their lorries as they had reached the number of miles they were permitted to drive without a rest.

Maxwell ate his breakfast and decided that if he was going to ask for a ride, it was now or never. He walked over to the table where the drivers were sitting.

'Excuse me but is anyone driving to the coast. I wonder if I could hitch a ride with someone who is going that way?' Maxwell held his breath while waiting for an answer.

'Where abouts do you want to go?' One of the lorry drivers was looking Maxwell up and down. He obviously didn't look like the average hitch hiker.

'I'm on my way to help a friend move his belongings to a new house, but unfortunately, my car has been taken back to the garage with engine trouble which will take some time to fix.

I don't want to let my friend down as he has helped me out on several occasions, so I told the garage I would try to hitch a lift.' Maxwell hoped that this story sounded reasonable.

After a short pause, one of the lorry drivers said, 'I'm going that way, if you can wait for half an hour, I will be able to start driving again.'

'That will be fine, I need to have a wash and brush up, what is the name on your lorry?'

The lorry driver gave him the name and registration number and Maxwell said 'Thank you' then made his way back to Laura's car.

He took both his holdalls out of the boot and decided to leave the car unlocked with the keys in the ignition. 'With a bit of luck someone might steal it and then the police might be tracking the wrong person?' He thought.

He went back to the restaurant and went into the washroom and quickly splashed some cold water on his face.

He looked at his wrist and realized he was wearing his Rolex watch, not something that a hitchhiker would have, he quickly took it off and slipped it in his pocket.

He made his way back to the lorry park and began to search for the registration number of the lorry to take him to the coast and hopefully find the town where Laura and Mia might be hiding.

'Who knows, after that he might be able to find someone to take him across the channel where he could catch a boat to take him and Mia back to his homeland?'

'I'm jumping too far ahead, let's just sort out one thing at a time.' He walked around looking at all the lorries until he found the right one. He took a deep breath and knocked on the side window.

CHAPTER THIRTY-ONE

Detective Conroy sat at his desk, the interview with Mr. Colin Burton had been playing on his mind.

He had arranged for Mr. Burton to have his DNA test which would take between 48 to 72 hours depending on the Scientist's workload. A post-mortem was due to take place soon and depending on the level of injuries to the body, that could take some-time.

Detective Conroy decided that he would bring Mr. Maxwell Hudson to the police station for an interview. 'I think it is time that this gentleman answered some questions. I think he is hiding something and the sooner I find out what it is, the better.'

He phoned his colleague. 'Hello Blakey, have you got time to come with me to Mr. Maxwell Hudson's house. I think I would like to bring him into the station for questioning. I'll meet you in the carpark.'

The two detectives drove to the large Detached house, set back from the road. They walked up the drive and the first thing they noticed was that one of the cars was missing.

They rang the doorbell and walked around the house peering in the windows. The back gate was unlocked so they went into the garden and knocked on the backdoor.

'Nobody seems to be home. I think the big Mercedes belongs to Mr. Hudson. Perhaps the silver Volvo belongs to his second wife.

She wasn't at home when we went to see him to tell him what had happened at Blackwell Road. Maybe they have both gone out in her car?

Perhaps we should put out an ANPR check. I wrote down both number plates when we were here last, just as a precaution in case he did a runner.

It was just something about his manner that day, he didn't seem that upset when we told him about the body that had been found.

Mr. Colin Burton seems convinced that Mr. Hudson had something to do with the disappearance of his daughter and I am beginning to think he could be right.

Let's get back to the station and do some searching. Mr. Hudson needs to be found and answer some questions.'

'Just a minute, look there is a lady in the front garden next door, why don't we have a quick word with her. Sometimes neighbours are quite knowledgeable about who lives next door to them, nosy is the word.' Detective Blake pointed to the next-door neighbour.

They walked over to the house, there was quite a distance between the two buildings.

'Good morning, may we have a few words with you if you have the time? Detective Conroy asked.

'Oh dear, I hope nothing dreadful has happened to anyone next door. I haven't seen Laura or Mia for some time, I was beginning to get worried about them.'

'Can I ask your name please? Detective Conway remembered that Maxwell had told him his wife and daughter were on a little holiday.

'I'm Mrs. Williams, what is this all about?' She looked upset.

'Have you seen the news about the house in Blackwell Road. I believe Mr. Hudson, your next-door neighbour, is the owner?'

'Yes, I believe he is. Apparently, he owns several houses in that part of town. Not a place I would want to live. Still, I think he is quite well off. Those old houses obviously bring in the money.'

'Do you have much to do with his wife and little girl?' asked Detective Conway.

'Not really, she doesn't seem to want to talk. She takes Mia to playschool twice a week.

If I'm in the front garden, I have in the past said, would she like to come in for a cup of coffee? She always says, she is in a hurry to get the washing done and has housework to do before she picks up Mia.

We did invite them to a barbecue once, but they never turned up, so we haven't bothered with them again. They are not very neighbourly.' Mrs. Williams shrugged her shoulders.

'I had my young granddaughter staying with me during the holidays some time ago and I said would Mia like to come and play with her, but Laura said Mia had a bad cold.

Mind you, I saw her taking Mia to playschool the next day.

It was if Laura wasn't allowed to have much to do with anyone in the road, and I can't remember her having any friends to visit. I should think she must have been quite lonely.

Her husband Mr. Hudson was much older than her,

maybe he didn't want her having anyone coming to the house?'

'The house seems empty today, the silver Volvo has gone. Was that the wife's car?' Detective Conway was beginning to get rather worried about Laura and her daughter.

'Yes, that belonged to Laura but as I said I haven't seen her for quite a while. I hope nothing has happened to her?'

'Well thank you for talking to us Mrs. Williams. If you do happen to see Mr. Hudson or Laura perhaps you would give us a ring. Here is my card if you feel you need to talk to me.'

He handed over the card and signaled to Blakey to make their way back to the car.

'I think I'll have a patrol car driving past a few times tonight to see if anyone is in the house, but after what Mrs. Williams has told us, I have a dreadful feeling something might have happened to his wife and daughter. The sooner we find him the better.'

CHAPTER THIRTY-TWO

Maxwell had found the lorry of the driver who had offered to give him a lift but there was no one sitting in the driver's seat. Luckily, he soon arrived and seemed in a hurry to get going.

'Just dump your luggage at the back of the seat there and we will be off.

My load is perishable, so I can't hang around for long. Where have you come from?' the driver looked at Maxwell.

'I had been driving for about 100 and fifty miles before my car gave out. I rang the break down company, and they took it away. I told them I was in a hurry to get to my friends and that I would hitch a ride.

It's very kind of you to give me a lift. Hope you won't get into any trouble for taking me in your lorry?'

'What they don't know, they won't have anything to worry about.' The driver smiled. 'My name is Jakub, what's yours?'

Maxwell had to think fast. 'My name is Dave Turner. I've been in this country for years, but I decided to change my name. My original one was not easy to pronounce.'

'Oh, what country do you come from? The driver smiled. 'I'm originally from Poland but I left there years ago.

I've had a much better life here and my children go to good schools, and I hope one day, because they have had a good education, they will be able to get a better job than a lorry driver.'

'My family come from a small Greek Island, and I thought I would stand a better life in England. I've never been back but I hope to go soon for a holiday.' Maxwell decided he wanted to change the subject.

'Do you do the same routes every week or does your company send you all round the country.' He asked.

'I mainly do the same route, but I do have plenty of time at home with my family, which is a perk of this job. Do you have children?'

Maxwell was beginning to regret hitch hiking, 'Yes, I have one daughter, who is away on holiday with my wife at the moment, so that is why I have got the time to go and help my friend to move.

I want to rent a van when we get to the coast, nothing too expensive, do you happen to know any garages where I could pick one up on the cheap?'

'Yes, I might be able to help you there. A mate of mine has a small garage, he could probably let you have one, how long would you want it for?'

'I'm planning to stay at my friend's house for a few days. He's going to need some help sorting all the furniture, carrying it up to the bedrooms etc. That would be a great help if you could drop me off near the garage?'

'That shouldn't be a problem, you just mention my name and I'm sure he will do you a deal?'

Maxwell was glad to change the subject. It was going to be a long journey.

'What are you carrying in the back, you said it was perishable?' Maxwell asked just to seem as if he was interested.

'It is meat, pork and poultry. There is a big meat processing plant up north, takes a few hours to get there, I have a rest while they are loading the lorry, I have to take at least 45 minutes off till I can drive again.

Then it's back on the road. I stop at the service station

and have some breakfast and by then I can get back to driving.'

'Would you mind very much if I shut my eyes and had a little sleep, I didn't get much last night, what with the car breaking down and everything?' Maxwell wanted to end the conversation.

'No, you go ahead, I am talking too much, being a lorry driver is a lonely job, sitting here driving for miles. It's nice to have someone to chat to.'

'I feel bad asking you now, but I am really tired. I won't be fit for much when I get to my friend's house if I don't get some shut eye.' Maxwell sat back in the seat and closed his eyes.

CHAPTER THIRTY-THREE

Laura was waiting at the front door for Adam to arrive. She had not been sleeping properly for several nights. She could not help wondering about Number 24 Blackwell Road. Something seemed to be praying on her mind.

She knew what Maxwell was capable of, when he was so vile to the poor woman and her child but surely, he had nothing to do with the human remains?

Luckily, Adam soon arrived, and Laura ran to his car and was impatient for him to open his door. As soon as he stood up, she flung her arms around him and hugged him tightly.

'That's a nice welcome' he smiled and had to stop himself from kissing her.

'I'm so glad to see you Adam, I've been looking out the

window for ages. I wish you lived nearer then we could see each during the week, Saturdays seem to be such a long time coming.'

'I wish I did too but maybe one day I'll be able to move to the coast, we shall just have to wait and see.' Saturdays could not come soon enough for him either. He loved the time that they spent together.

'Come on in, let's sit down and have a talk, there are a few things I want to tell you.' Laura led the way indoors.

'Jacky is busy at work on Saturdays at her Hair Salon, so we have got all day. We can go out later.

Mia is in the garden but as soon as she realizes that you have arrived, we won't have a quiet moment to talk.' Laura laughed. 'Can I get you a cup of coffee?'

'Not just yet, sit down and tell me how you are?' Adam was worried about Laura. She was looking so very tired.

'I'm not sleeping very well, I keep thinking about the body at 24 Blackwell Road, wondering if Maxwell did have something to do with it?' Laura looked as if she was about to burst into tears.

Adam put his arm around her, pulling her close. 'I just wish I could do something to put your mind at rest.

I'm sure we will soon hear on the news if they have identified the body and how long it had been buried for. It could have been in the ground for years.'

'I know you are right, but I can't stop remembering how dreadful Maxwell was when that poor woman and her child came to the house, it was then that I saw for the first time, exactly what he is capable of.'

'Well hopefully it won't be too long before the police have some evidence to arrest someone, and then you'll have nothing to worry about.

Let's talk about something else. The bungalow is nearly ready to put up for sale.

Have you thought where you would like to live once the sale goes through?' Adam was hoping that she might move nearer to him.

'Not really, I shall be sad when we have to sell it. Mia and I have been so happy here these last few months.

Being by the seaside has helped to lift my spirits and Mia has had a lovely time. She hardly ever says anymore, when is her father coming to see us? I think she loves living here as much as I do.'

'I don't think you will have much trouble selling it quickly, it looks really lovely now.'

Adam wished he had enough money to buy Jacky's half, then Laura wouldn't have to move out.

He was falling in love with Laura and was beginning to

hope that they might have a future together.

'Mia will soon be 4 years old and will have to go to primary school. So, we will have to start looking for one once the bungalow is sold and I will have to find somewhere else to live.

Here she comes in from the garden, let's get ready and go down to the beach. It's a lovely day and we might as well make the most of the time we have left, before we have to move.'

CHAPTER THIRTY-FOUR

'Mr. Burton, we have the results of your DNA Test and I wondered if you could come to the Police station this afternoon at 2.00pm?'

Detective Conroy was not looking forward to seeing Mr. Burton again. 'Have you someone that you would like to bring with you?'

When Mr. Burton replied that there was no one who could accompany him, Detective Conroy said never mind, he would have someone here to sit with him.

Detective Conroy rang through to the next office. 'Blakey would you please come and sit in on the interview this afternoon with Mr. Burton.

I have just been speaking to him. I've asked him to come and get the results of his DNA Test. He says he has no one to accompany him, that's why I'm asking you to sit in.'

'Yes, I'll be there, what time do you want me.' Detective Blake already knew the results and felt sorry for the old man.

'Perhaps we should also have someone else. The Family Liaison Worker could sit in, in case the old man is taken ill, suggested Blakey.

'I think you are right. I'll get on to that now.' Detective Conroy was not looking forward to this meeting. 'I've asked him to come here at 2.00pm.

At the appointed time, Mr. Burton arrived at the Police station. Detective Conroy came to collect him from Reception.

'Would you like something to drink Mr. Burton. A cup of tea or coffee perhaps?

'No thank you, I would just like you to tell me as quickly as possible, the result of the test. My mind has been full of nothing else for days.

I haven't been sleeping properly and I just have the feeling that it isn't going to be good news.' Mr. Burton was shaking and near to tears.

'Let us go and sit in my office. I've asked Detective Blake and a Family Liaison worker to sit in with us.'

They reached the office and when everyone was seated, Detective Conroy began to speak.

'Very well Mr. Burton. The DNA test on you and the remains found at 24 Blackwell Road, have definitely proved that you and the body are a perfect match.

I am so sorry Mr. Burton, but sadly it does mean it is your daughter.' Detective Conroy took a deep breath and sat looking at the poor man opposite.

Mr. Burton's face gave nothing away, he was silently taking in the information that he had just been told.

'I suppose I knew what you were going to tell me. My daughter would not have run away and gone abroad, without telling my wife and myself.

She would never have put her mother through so much agony not knowing where she was. At least now, I can give her a proper funeral.

I think I would like to know how my daughter was killed.' Mr. Burton seemed in some way relieved that he finally knew what had happened to his daughter.

'Are you sure Mr. Burton? You might find it too upsetting, perhaps we should wait until another time?'

'No, I would like to know now, I will only be imagining the worst.'

'The coroner was given the post-mortem results and the

cause of death was murder.

Sadly, your daughter was strangled.' Detective Conroy knew he would have to tell Mr. Burton sometime, but it was not a part of his job that he looked forward to.

Mr. Burton gave out a cry of anguish. 'Well, now you can arrest Maxwell Hudson, I knew all along that he was behind my daughter's disappearance.

I hope the bastard rots in jail for the rest of his life.' He began to sob uncontrollably.

'I am so very sorry Mr. Burton, but Maxwell Hudson has absconded. We went to check on his house, but he hasn't been seen for several days. We have had a patrol car driving past in the evenings but there has been no sign that anyone has been living there.

The silver Volvo that was parked on the drive is missing. We checked the driver's records, and that car belongs to his wife.

A neighbour told us that she has not seen his wife or little girl for weeks maybe months. Maxwell told us that his wife and daughter were on a little holiday. It would seem strange if that were true, if it is so, why didn't she take her car?'

'Oh my god, I hope he hasn't harmed them.' Mr. Burton sat with his head bowed.

'We have put Mr. Hudson's description on the Police National Computer saying that he is wanted for the disappearance of his first wife.

The body found at 24 Blackwell Road has been identified as Julia Hudson who has been missing for 12 years. This is now a homicide investigation.'

'Let's hope you soon catch up with him.' Mr. Burton stood up. He caught hold of the arm of the chair and just caught himself before he fell over. 'I think I would like to go home now. I don't feel very well. I think the shock has been too much.'

'I will get some-one to take you home Mr. Burton.' The Family Liaison worker took him by the arm.

'You can be sure that we are determined to catch him and bring him to justice, you can count on that. We will be keeping you updated of any progress. If you want to contact me at any time, please do.'

Detective Blake walked out with him to Reception and arrangements were made for him to be taken home. He returned to Detective Conroy's office.

'Well Blakey, that poor old fellow. That's not an interview I would like to do again. All these years he hasn't known where his daughter was and now, he will have to arrange her funeral.'

'It least he will have some sort of closure. When we find Maxwell, there will be a trial, that will be very hard on the old man.

It least we know exactly why he has absconded, although I think we already knew. Let's get going, the faster we find him, the better.'

CHAPTER THIRTY-FIVE

'Well, this is as far as I can take you. I think I will drop you off here. The friend who has the garage is not too far away. You can walk there in about twenty minutes.

Tell him that Jakub sent you and I'm sure he will be able to do a deal for you?'

'You have been very kind, thank you so much. I'm not sure what I would have done if you had not offered to help me. Here's a few pounds for your trouble.' Maxwell held out his hand and gave Jakub a couple of twenty-pound notes.'

'You don't have to do that, but it is very good of you.' Jakub shook his hand. 'I hope the friend is grateful for you coming all this way to help with the house removal?'

'Oh, we have been friends for years and he has helped

me out several times, so I owe him one.'

Maxwell picked up the two black holdalls from the back of his seat and climbed down the step onto the pavement. 'Thank you once again, take care.'

Jakub had given him the address of the garage and Maxwell began to walk in that direction.

He was hoping that the garage had an old van that he could buy rather than rent. He had decided to look for the address where Laura's aunt had lived and maybe park and wait to see whether Laura and Mia were at that address.

Eventually he reached the Garage. He quickly looked around the forecourt where second- hand cars and a few vans were parked.

There was a white van that looked as if it might be possible for his needs. The price was reasonable for the year of manufacture. It was about 10 years old.

A man came out of the office and said, 'Hello, is there anything I can do to help you with?'

'Good morning, I have been talking to a friend of yours, Jakub. He gave me the address of your garage.

He thought you might have a van for me as I am looking for one. I have told a mate that I will help move his furniture into his new house.

I was just looking at this one here. Could you tell me

something about it?'

'Oh, Jakub is a good friend of mine. How is he?'

'He's fine, he gave me a lift down here when my motor broke down. It was very kind of him.' Maxwell was impatient to get on with the transaction.

'This Transit Van has a high mileage but has been well looked after. It's got six months Mot.'

'How much are you asking for it?' Maxwell just wanted the deal to be done.

'Well as you can see, I've got it up for £1500.' The owner of the garage stood looking at Maxwell.

'I can give you cash for it, so you won't have to put it through the books.' Maxwell stood waiting for an answer.

'I don't think I can do that?' The owner was not sure about this man. Was he someone who was trying to trick him into breaking the law?

'What if I give you Two thousand for it and no questions asked?' Maxwell took a deep breath.

The owner stood for a while, obviously thinking should he take the risk, then said 'Well okay but you didn't get it from me, if anyone asks? You must be desperate to help your friend.'

'I will not be telling anyone you can be sure of that. Can I use your toilet, I was in Jakub's lorry for hours? Perhaps you can get the Van ready to drive away while I'm in there?'

'Okay, the toilet is at the back of my office. I'll get the keys to the van and get the V5 ready.'

Maxwell made his way to the toilet and opened the holdall which contained the cash. He counted out Two thousand pounds in fifty-pound notes. He looked at himself in the mirror.

He needed a shave, and his eyes looked tired. He zipped up the holdall and made his way back outside.

'Here you are, I'll count it out for you.' Maxwell handed it over and stood waiting for the keys.

'Very nice doing business with you. Next time I see Jakub, I will thank him for sending you here.' The owner smiled at Maxwell and stood waiting for him to go.

Maxwell climbed into the driving seat and turned the key. Luckily, the engine started first time.

'Thanks a lot, I'll be on my way.' Maxwell drove off and stopped at the nearest garage and filled the van with diesel. He bought himself something to eat and found a local map.

'Right, all I have to do now is find the bungalow. I've already got the address.

I think I will have a little rest, then study the map while I'm having something to eat.' He drove to where he could park and sit looking out to sea.

'I'm feeling so tired, perhaps I will find a Bed and Breakfast to stay for a couple of nights while I try and make some plans on how I am going to get out of the country. Maybe the Police have already alerted the Airports and Train Stations.'

Maxwell spread out the local map and after a while he found the road he was looking for. He then had something to eat and soon after he fell asleep.

CHAPTER THIRTY-SIX

Hi Blakey, I've just had a long conversation with the Motorway Police. They spotted Mrs. Laura Hudson's silver Volvo on the M1 Motorway and pulled it over.

Sadly, Maxwell Hudson wasn't driving it. A young lad said he had found it abandoned a short distance from the Service Station on the M1.

The lad had been out with a couple of mates on a joy ride in one of their parent's cars.

Apparently, the mother and father are away on holiday, so they had 'borrowed' it.

They had come across the Silver Volvo parked down a side road. The lad had got out of their car and walked over to have a look at it. He saw the keys had been left in the ignition and his friends dared him to take it for a drive.

'I wonder if Maxwell was meeting someone at the Service Station. Maybe he had rung a friend to come and pick him up.'

'I don't think so Blakey. I expect he realized we would have written down the Registration number when we were at his house. I imagine he just wanted to get rid of it.'

Detective Conroy continued 'The young lad is in custody and is being questioned further. He was also driving without a licence and no insurance.'

'Perhaps it is a good thing that this lad stole the car. At least we know how far Maxwell had driven it.'

Detective Conroy nodded his head. 'I've sent a photograph of Maxwell to the Motorway Police and asked them to go to the Service Station and show it around. Someone must have seen him. Perhaps he had breakfast there?'

'That's a good idea. You never know maybe a Lorry driver gave him a lift?'

'Well at least we have something to go on. He must have driven about 100 and fifty miles from his home. I wonder where he is headed?'

'The fact that he immediately did a runner proves he knew the body that was found at Blackwell Road was his first wife and that he killed her.'

'I have been doing some checks and he hasn't taken any money out of his bank account or used his mobile phone. He must have had plenty of money stashed away in his house?'

'It's time Blakey that we get a search warrant and have a good look around his house. Maybe we can find something that will give us an idea where he has gone?'

'Right, the sooner the better. There must be something in the house that will give us a clue as to the whereabouts of his wife and child. Hopefully, they are somewhere safe.'

CHAPTER THIRTY-SEVEN

Maxwell rose from his sleep with a start. For a few moments he didn't know where he was.

He sat looking out to sea. 'I need to find a boat that can take me at least over to France and then maybe I can make my way back to Greece.'

He pulled out the map he had bought and the piece of paper that he had written the road and number of the house where Aunt Mabel lived.

'I think I had better find a bed and breakfast for tonight. There will be plenty of time in the morning to work out exactly what I am going to do next.'

He looked at the map again and started to drive round the town looking for a sign showing a bed and breakfast hotel.

It was a seaside town so there were plenty of B and Bs to choose from, but Maxwell didn't want a fancy one that might have lots of bedrooms, he just needed a small one where he wouldn't need to have conversations with the other guests.

He soon came across a detached house that looked rather run down and decided that he would park on the front drive and see if there was a room vacant for him to stay the night.

He put on his dark glasses and took the two holdalls from the back of the van. He suddenly thought he had better make a note of the registration number, thinking that he might have to write it down when he booked in.

He walked in the front door and made his way to a desk where a lady was sitting reading a magazine.

'Excuse me, but I am looking for a room for the night and breakfast in the morning?'

The lady rose to her feet and looked Maxwell up and down. 'Certainly sir. We have a couple of spare rooms. One of them has a bathroom with a shower, so that costs a little more than the one that hasn't.

There is a bathroom along the corridor, but I expect you will be more comfortable in the one with its own facilities.' She smiled at Maxwell. He looked rather better dressed than some of her customers.

'That will be fine. I'm rather tired so all I want to do is get some rest. Do you have Wi-fi here I need to do some work on my laptop?'

'Well, we have but sometimes it does play up a bit. Would you like to sign in and then I can show you to your room?'

Maxwell signed in as Dave Turner, a name that had suddenly come to him while in the lorry with Jakub. He wrote down the registration number of the van in the space provided.

'Just follow me sir, your room is on the second floor, if there is anything you need, just ring down and I will bring it up to you. Are you sure I can't get you anything to eat?'

'No thank you, I had something not very long ago, but I would like a full English breakfast in my room in the morning, if that is possible?'

'What time would you like it?'

'About 8am. Well good night, I just need a rest. I've driven a long way today.' Maxwell opened the door with the key she had given him and quickly shut it.

He sat down on the bed and looked around him. He was used to lovely expensive hotels not this horrible bedroom with faded wallpaper and the smell of disinfectant.

He stood up and opened the door to the bathroom. Well at least he had a shower. He looked at his watch. 'I'll just plug in my laptop and see if I can find the news channel, hopefully there is nothing about 24 Blackwell Road?'

He sat reading the news and sighed with relief when he found nothing that caused him anxiety.

'I'll just have a look at the Town Centre and work out where I want to go tomorrow.' He soon found the bungalow that he was hoping might be the place where Laura and Mia were living.

He also found the Marina. 'Maybe there might be a boat which could take me across the Channel to France?' He switched off his laptop and made his way to the bathroom.

He had a shower with tepid water and flopped into bed, exhausted by the worry of the past day and was soon fast asleep.

CHAPTER THIRTY-EIGHT

'You know I sent Maxwell's photo to the Security people at the service station, on the M1 where Laura's car was found?

Well, I asked if they could send me some of the security tapes from early that morning. Do you want to come and watch them with me?'

'I'll be there in about five minutes, don't start without me.'

Detective Conroy set up the CCTV and settled down ready to watch it when Blakey arrived.

They both sat staring intently at the screen. There were pictures of the Entrance to the shops and the Restaurant.

Suddenly Detective Conroy sat bolt upright, stopped the film, and stared at the figure paying for a meal at the counter.

'I think that's him. Let's zoom in on to his face. He has obviously shaved off his beard to try and disguise himself, that's why he's wearing dark glasses and a baseball cap.

Look at the cap, there is a logo on the front, it's the sign for Mercedes cars. Got you!' Conroy stood up and punched the air.

Blakey said, 'Let's keep watching, we might be able to see him talking to some-one?'

They started to watch the film again and it showed that Maxwell carried his breakfast tray to a table near a group of men. He sat down to eat and when he had finished his meal, he walked over to the table where the men were sitting and stood there talking to them.

'Do you think those men are Lorry drivers. They are all wearing different overalls possibly with the name of their Companies Logos. I think that Maxwell is trying to hitch a lift somewhere?' Blakey wondered.

'Let's go back to the moment where Maxwell pays for his breakfast and turns towards the camera. We can get a photo from the still, then we will have the image of how he looks now he has shaved his beard off.' Detective Conroy said staring at the screen.

'That's a good idea, then we can circulate the photo to

Airports, Ferries, and Train Stations.' Agreed Blakey.

'I think he may be headed towards the South Coast. Maybe he is trying to get across the Channel. We need to find him before he disappears.

I feel so sorry for Mr. Burton. He needs to know that Maxwell will be punished for what he has done to his daughter. Right, we better get going, we've got plenty to do.

Hopefully, there may be a clue at the Hudson house as to where his wife Laura and his daughter Mia are? We need to find them before Maxwell does.'

CHAPTER THIRTY-NINE

'Hi Blakey, I've told the locksmith to meet us at the Hudson House. Will you be ready to leave in about 10 minutes?

The patrol car has been driving past the house several times during the night but has reported no sign that anyone is living there.'

'I must admit I am looking forward to searching the house. Hopefully, we might find clues to the whereabouts of his wife and the little girl? I keep wondering where they are?'

'Right, Blakey, see you in the carpark. The sooner we get this search underway the better. Maxwell Hudson is obviously on the run because he is guilty of murdering his first wife.'

They drove to Maxwell's house. The Mercedes was still parked on the drive.

Detective Conroy got out of the car and was about to walk over to the locksmith, when a voice called out, 'Hello Detective Conroy.'

It was the next-door neighbour, Mrs. Williams. She was making her way across her garden.

'Good morning, Mrs. Williams, how are you today?' Detective Conroy stood waiting for her as she reached the hedge separating the gardens.

'I'm so glad to see you.' She was breathing rather quickly. 'I've been keeping a watch on the house and I'm sure no one has been there, only the postman.'

'Thank you very much for keeping watch. We have come here today with a Search Warrant.

The locksmith is going to open the back door for us.'

'Well, I hope you will find some clue to the whereabouts of Laura and Mia? I've been very upset worrying about them.'

'We will be searching the whole house. You told us you haven't seen either of them for weeks maybe months?'

'Oh, I do hope they are alright. You will let me know if you find them, won't you?'

'It could take some time to locate them. I suppose there

is a possibility, they might have gone abroad, if we do find them, then I will definitely let you know.

Well, we had better get on with the search, it's going to take some time as the house is so large.'

'Please don't let me slow you down.' Mrs. Williams made her way back to her front door.

'Well, Blakey, we had better get going, here comes the locksmith.'

Two Constables arrived to help them with the search. As soon as the back door was opened, Detective Conroy said, 'Blakey, you and a Constable start looking upstairs, and I will do the same down here.'

He made his way along the corridor to the study where they had interviewed Maxwell.

He opened the door and the first thing he saw was the open safe on the wall.

'It's empty, he's obviously taken the contents with him.' He began to pull open the drawers in the desk. He emptied them onto the floor and knelt down. He carefully went through the contents.

One file had the names and addresses of the houses and names of the people who were renting the properties that Maxwell owned.

Detective Conroy called to one of the Constables and

together they put the file into a plastic bag to take with them to the Police Station.

Another file had the details of Laura's Family Tree. Detective Conroy began to read the report from a firm called Albright and Thomson.

One name had been circled in pen, a Mr. Charles Mortimer. It had his home address. 'Maybe this might lead to the whereabouts of Laura and her daughter.' He put this file in another plastic bag.

He decided to make his way upstairs. 'Blakey, I've found a couple of documents that might be useful. How are you doing up here?'

'I've found something which is giving me concern. Come and look at this?' Blakey opened a black dustbin bag. Inside were bundles of women's clothes that had been torn to shreds.

'Look at the floor over there by the dressing table, someone has smashed glass bottles and China ornaments all over the carpet. One of the big wardrobes is completely empty and the other one is full of expensive suits and shirts.'

'It doesn't look very good for the wife, does it? I wonder what has happened to her. I've got the name of a cousin called Charles Mortimer. I think we should go and have a talk with him as soon as possible.'

The search of the whole house took some time but as soon as they had completed it, the locksmith put a new lock on the back door and handed over the keys.

'Let's go back to the Station and hand over the files of the people living in Maxwell's houses but first I want to find Charles Mortimer. Hopefully Laura might be living there and then perhaps we will know that she and her daughter are safe.'

CHAPTER FORTY

'Mr. Charles Mortimer?'

'Yes, who are you?'

'My name is Detective Conroy, and this is Detective Blake. We would like to ask you some questions about a Mr. Maxwell Hudson.

Have you seen this gentleman lately? Here is a photograph. Would you please take a good look and tell us if you know him?'

Mr. Mortimer took the photograph and stared at it. 'I'm not likely to forget this gentleman, if you could call him that, he burst into my house and ran around calling out for his wife.

He told me that she was my cousin and that for some reason, he thought I was hiding her here.'

'How long ago did this happen? You see he has gone missing and is wanted for a very serious crime.' Detective Conroy asked.

'Well, I'm not exactly sure when it was. I was frightened and told him I was going to call the police. Luckily when he had finished looking in all the rooms, he charged out of the door, jumped in his car and drove off at speed.'

'It would help if you could tell us approximately when this happened. We are also very worried that something dreadful might have happened to his wife Laura and her daughter Mia.'

Detective Conroy took back the photograph and stood waiting for Mr. Mortimer to answer.

'I think it was about three months ago, it took me a long time to get over the shock, I always put the chain on the front door now before I open it to anyone.'

'Did you report it to the Police?'

'Well, I didn't think it was worth bothering them. He didn't steal anything and luckily he has never been back.'

'Thank you for your time, Mr. Mortimer. At least it would appear that Maxwell Hudson doesn't know where his wife has gone? Maybe, she has run away from him and taken her little girl. We just hope that they are somewhere safe?'

Detective Conroy and Detective Blake made their way back to their car. 'I wonder where his wife and daughter are?

Someone must be hiding them. I just hope we can find them before he does?'

'Perhaps we should have another look at her family tree that might have some clues where she has gone. She has a sister called Jacky, maybe if we could find her, perhaps she is hiding them?'

'Well, the family tree is with the other papers we took from the house. Maxwell might be trying to find his wife. Maybe if we could find Laura, he might be somewhere in the same vicinity?'

'Right, let's make our way back to the station and see if we can figure out where Maxwell was headed when he left his car at that Service Station?'

CHAPTER FORTY-ONE

Maxwell awoke with a start, for a few seconds he didn't know where he was.

He sat up in bed and stared around him. 'What a hovel, the sooner I find someone to take me across the Channel the better.

Maybe I shouldn't spend too much time trying to find Laura, it will only put me in danger of being arrested.'

He got out of bed and made his way to the bathroom. He quickly shaved and had a shower. The water was tepid but that was the least of his worries. He looked at his watch, 7.30am, he had asked for his breakfast to be delivered to his room at 8.0am.

He dressed and turned on his laptop. He looked at the News Channel and was glad to see there was no mention of

No. 24 Blackwell Road. He sighed with relief. His plan today was to find the Marina and maybe get a passage over to France.

There was a knock on the door. 'Mr. Turner, I've got your breakfast, would you like me to leave it outside your door or are you up and dressed.'

Maxwell opened the door. It was the same woman that was on Reception last night. She stood there smiling at him.

'Thank you very much, I'll take it from here.' He took the tray and quickly closed the door before she had the time to engage him in any conversation.

He sat down at the small table and uncovered the meal. It didn't look too bad although the bacon was rather greasy, but he was hungry and soon he had eaten the whole plateful. The coffee was obviously rather cheap and nasty but what did he expect in this rundown hotel.

'The sooner I find a way to get out of the country the better.' He looked out of the window to see what the weather was doing.

It was rather misty but at least it wasn't raining, he quickly got together the things he would need to take with him.

He put his laptop in the holdall with the money and decided to leave the other one in the room. He would probably have to spend another night here while he tried to make some plans for him to leave the country.

He put on his baseball hat and dark glasses and made his way downstairs, luckily no one else seemed to be around.

He quickly said thank you for his breakfast and said he had left the tray outside his room.

He made his way to the van and sat inside having a last look at the map and drove off in search of the Marina.

Maybe he might find a boat that he could buy, after all someone might have seen his photo and recognized him.

The fewer people he had to talk to the better. He had done some sailing when he was young, surely, he could find his way to the Channel and then to France.

CHAPTER FORTY-TWO

Laura sat having her breakfast while watching the morning news on television. Suddenly a picture of No. 24 Blackwell Drive came on the screen. She stopped eating and sat still staring at the house.

A newsreader was standing outside. 'The human remains that were found in the garden of No. 24 have been identified as Julia Burton, she was the first wife of Maxwell Hudson.

The coroner has listed the death as murder and Mr. Maxwell Hudson is wanted for questioning.

We have a recent photograph that was taken at a service station on the M1. If anybody has any information about the whereabouts of Maxwell Hudson, will they contact their local Police Station.'

Laura looked at the photograph. It was Maxwell but he had shaved off his beard. She sat shaking and was finding it difficult to breath.

Who should she ring? Adam or Jacky, or maybe both. She decided to ring Adam.

'Hello Laura, are you alright, is there anything wrong?' Adam sounded concerned. Laura never usually rang him at work.

'Adam I've just been watching the news. Maxwell is wanted for murder. The body at 24 Blackwell Road has been identified as Maxwell's first wife.' Laura began to sob.

'Oh my god, I'm so sorry, you must be so frightened. Surely, he wouldn't come anywhere near you if the Police are looking for him.

He will be trying to escape somewhere. Do you want me to come down, I can tell work that someone is ill, and I will need the day off?'

'No, don't do that, I will be alright, I think I will take Mia to her playschool, I will feel better that she is somewhere that is safe.'

'What will you be doing? I don't want you sitting in the bungalow all day worrying. As soon as I finish work, I will come straight down.'

'I'm going to ring Jacky next and tell her. She will

221

probably come and sit with me.'

'Well, if you are sure. I will come straight from work. I love you, Laura.' That was the first time Adam had said those three little words.

'I love you too Adam. See you tonight.' Laura sat thinking about what Adam had just said to her. She knew he was fond of her but was so happy to know that his feelings were the same as hers.

She rang Jacky. 'I am so sorry to bother you at work, but I've just seen on the news that Maxwell is wanted by the Police for the murder of his first wife'

'What! Do you want me to come home? Are you frightened?

'I suppose I am more in shock than anything. Surely, he doesn't know where I am If he did, he would have turned up here long before now?

I think I will still take Mia to playschool. She will be safe there. I don't want her to see the news on the television.

I suppose it will be in all the papers. I'll drop her off and do my shift at the Café. At least I will be with people all day.'

'Maybe that would be the right thing to do at least you will have something to take your mind off what is happening.

I'll be home right after work, and we can have a talk to see if you should contact the local Police.'

'I know this sounds silly, but can we have a code word that if I say it, will mean he has found me. It could be anything that could fit into a sentence, what do you think?'

'I don't think that's silly if it makes you feel safe. What about a little girl's name?'

'How about 'Rebecca' maybe I could fit that into a sentence?'

'Right, if you ring me and mention 'Rebecca' I will know that there is something wrong but I'm sure he doesn't know where you are, please try not to worry.'

'Right, I'll get Mia up and make sure to turn off the television and the radio. See you tonight?'

Laura kept thinking of the story that Maxwell had told her about his first wife.

He had said she had run away with her boyfriend to live abroad. It had obviously been a lie. She shuddered when she thought she had believed him and that she had been living with a murderer.

Obviously, she would have to talk to the police, but not yet. Hopefully, they would soon catch up with Maxwell and lock him up. Perhaps then she would finally feel safe.

CHAPTER FORTY-THREE

Laura let Mia play in the garden for a little while before getting her ready for bed. Laura wanted to talk to Jacky, but she didn't want Mia to overhear what she had heard on the television.

'Jacky, I knew he was a bad man, but I never dreamed he was a murderer. Do you think we should go to the Police and let them know where I am. They might think that Mia and I are with him?' Laura was near to tears.

'I don't know what to say to you Laura. After all we are still hoping that he doesn't know where you are. Surely the Police are looking all over the country, Maxwell could be anywhere.'

'What do you think Adam, what would you do if you were me?' Laura looked at Adam. The last words he had spoken to her on the phone, were 'I love you.'

'It is difficult to know the best way to handle this. I just want him to be caught and sent to prison, then you will never have to worry about him ever again. You will be free to do what you want for the rest of your life. I hate to see you living like this, always looking over your shoulder.' Adam wished he could be of more help.

'I think the best thing to do, is try and carry on as normal. Mia will be safe at playschool, no one is allowed to pick her up in the afternoon except me or you Laura, so there is no way he could kidnap her.

He could be anywhere. He could even have managed to leave the country by now. Why would he stay here when he could be halfway across the world?' Jacky was trying to sound positive.

'Would you like me to have time off work, Laura? I could stay here and make sure you are protected.' Adam felt helpless, he couldn't bear to think that something might happen to Laura and Mia.

'No, Adam, I don't think that is necessary at the moment. Surely the Police will catch up with him before long?

I just want to protect Mia. Luckily, I don't think she has seen any of the news on television. I just want to keep her life as normal as possible. The children she mixes with at playschool, will not be saying anything to her about her Daddy, they are too young. It would be different if she was older, then she might realize what is happening.

'Let's get her in from the garden and have a lovely tea and we can play some games before she is ready for bed.' Adam stood up and went into the garden and swung Mia up onto his shoulders and pretended to be a horse galloping around the garden. Mia was laughing and Laura stood looking out the kitchen window at them both.

She thought that the day Adam came to the boot fair was like a fairy tale, it was if he was her Prince Charming. She felt so lucky that he was now part of her life and that Mia loved him as much as she did.

Soon it was time for Mia to go to bed and Laura tucked her up with Bunny and kissed her goodnight.

'I did suggest to Jacky, that if Maxwell did find me and Mia, that I would try to phone her and say a secret code name. I decided on 'Rebecca'. I thought I might be able to get this name into a sentence without Maxwell realizing what I was doing.

Maybe I could say that Mia had been invited to a Birthday Party and that we would be late home. Do you think that might be a good idea, Adam?'

'Yes, I do, it's a good idea to have something prepared just in case the worst happens, but I hope you will never have to use it.' Adam sighed.

'Well, I think I will drive home now. Don't forget you can phone me anytime you like. I'll be down again tomorrow, hopefully there will be some good news that Maxwell is in custody.'

Laura walked to the front door with him. 'Thank you for coming down, it was very kind of you.'

Adam took her in his arms and for the first time he did something he had wanted to do for months, he kissed her.

'I love you Laura and hopefully when this nightmare is over, I want to marry you. Do you think you might want to marry me.?'

'Yes, Adam. I love you too and hopefully one of these days we can be together.'

Laura stood by the door and watched Adam drive away. How she wished she had met Adam before she had married Maxwell but there was no good looking back.

CHAPTER FORTY-FOUR

Maxwell drove towards the town and decided to park down a side street. He was longing for a decent cup of coffee.

He made his way along the high street and stopped at a café and bought himself a drink. He walked along sipping his coffee and stopped at a Newsagents. The morning papers were displayed outside on a rack and Maxwell stood looking at them.

One paper had a headline. 'Body found at 24 Blackwell Road identified.' See page 4.

Maxwell picked up the paper and turned to page 4. There was a photograph of him. 'It must have been taken from the footage on a CCTV camera at the Service Station.

I will have to buy myself some new clothes. I am

wearing the exact clothes I was wearing yesterday. Thank God I left when I did. I would be in custody by now.

I had better find a way to get across the Channel as soon as possible.'

He hurriedly put back the paper and saw there was a rubbish bin outside the shop. He took off his baseball hat and threw it in the bin. He continued to walk along the high street and luckily came across a clothes shop selling sailing gear.

He went in and started to look along the racks. What should he buy first? Perhaps a navy-blue waterproof jacket, a striped long sleaved sweatshirt and some deck shoes would be useful. He found the right sizes to try on and took them into the changing room.

He took off the clothes he was wearing and tried on the items he had taken off the rails. They fitted perfectly and Maxwell decided to keep them on. He added up the prices and took out the cash from the holdall.

He walked back into the shop and an assistant spoke to him. 'Are you happy with the clothes you have tried on sir?

'Yes, they are just what I was looking for. A friend is going to take me sailing today so I thought I might as well look the part. Have you got a bag that I can put the clothes I was wearing into?'

The assistant found a large bag and Maxwell bungled the clothes into it. 'Have you got a hat I could wear? It will probably be rather windy out at sea.'

'Well, your waterproof jacket has got a hood. If you want to sunbath on deck while you are stationary, you could wear a straw Panama hat, I think you would look very smart in one. They do come in navy.'

The assistant stood smiling at Maxwell.

'That sounds like a good idea. Where are they?' Maxwell looked around the store.

'I'll get one for you sir, what size hat do you take?'

'Medium should be large enough, thank you.' Maxwell thought 'I could pull a hat down over my eyes, it would help cover my face.'

The assistant soon found one and began to add up the bill. 'How will you be paying for all this sir, Cash or Card?'

'Cash, I've just been to the machine.' Maxwell counted out the total in twenty-pound notes.

'Well, I hope you have a lovely day sailing with your friend.' The assistant smiled at Maxwell as he turned to leave the shop.

As soon as Maxwell found a large rubbish bin, he dropped in the bag full of the clothing he had been wearing. He gazed into the window of the shop nearby and was pleased with his new appearance. The only item he did not throw away, were his sunglasses.

'I think it is time I made my way to the Marina, at least I look the part now. The sooner I find a way to disappear, the better.'

CHAPTER FORTY-FIVE

Maxwell made his way across town and saw the sign for the Marina.

He parked up a side road and decided to walk the rest of the way. He took his black holdall full of the money with him.

He began to walk up and down the rows of different types of craft. There were plenty of yachts moored up, but Maxwell was looking for a Cabin Cruiser.

He wanted a boat which could get up some speed and not be reliant on the wind.

As he walked up and down the rows of boats, he suddenly stopped and stood looking at a 'For Sale' sign notice next to a Cabin Cruiser.

The boat in front of him looked a good size. There was

a telephone number to ring on the notice board saying that if you were interested to call, and Maxwell was just about to do so, when someone tapped him on the shoulder.

'Excuse me sir, but are you about to ring my mobile?'

Maxwell turned and looked at the man beside him. 'Yes, I was, are you the owner of this boat?'

'I am and it is up for sale as I have decided I am getting too old to go sailing on my own.

The wife was never a good sailor, she usually spent most of the time onboard in the bedroom lying down, while we were at sea.

Sadly, my wife died six months ago and frankly it is not as much fun without her.' He sighed.

'So sorry to hear that. I expect you miss her a great deal. I used to do some sailing in my youth but have been too busy with my work to have time for hobbies.

I have now decided to retire, so that I can begin to enjoy life again.' Maxwell thought this could be the opportunity he was looking for.

'Would you like to come onboard and have a look around. She is in extremely good order. I always keep the engine well maintained.

My name is Richard Burrows by the way.' He put out his hand to shake Maxwell's.

'It is strange how we always refer to boats as 'she' I have never really thought why that is.'

'That's a strong grip you have there, must be tying up the ropes and swabbing down the decks.' Maxwell laughed.

'My name is Dave Turner. It is very nice to meet you, I would love to see onboard.' Maxwell said smiling.

Richard led the way, 'We are able to just jump onboard docked here in the Marina. I shall be sad to let her go. I named her after my wife, 'Christina.'

'I think that was a lovely thing to do, I'm sure she appreciated having a boat named after her, quite an honour.' Maxwell stood on the deck and began to look around him. 'How many cabins does it have below?'

'Well, there is one double and a small single, but we always found it plenty big enough for us.' Richard smiled.

'That should be quite adequate. My wife and I can share the double and my little girl can sleep in the single. Can I have a look below?' Maxwell was in a hurry to see exactly what condition the boat was in.

'Certainly, of course she was second hand when I purchased her seven years ago. A new version of this model was way too expensive for me.

We had some lovely holidays just sailing around the British Isles. She had a different name when I purchased her, so we had to have a special ceremony when we changed her name.

We invited some friends and family. Apparently, it is bad luck to change the name of a boat, so we had a 'Purging Ceremony' to appease 'The Four Winds Gods.'

A load of rubbish really, but we all enjoyed ourselves and smashed a cheap bottle of Champagne on the bow and drank the expensive one.' Richard laughed. 'You might want to change the name again into your wife's.'

'I don't think I will do that, don't want to upset the Gods.' Maxwell laughed.

'Hurry up man, I just want to see the rest of the boat.' Maxwell said to himself, trying to contain his frustration.

Richard showed him the galley and the bathroom. The main cabin was a good size, and the smaller one Maxwell thought would be fine for Mia.

'Is it possible for you to take me for a little sail. I would like to hear the engine running and perhaps you would let me steer for a while?'

Maxwell did not want to take too much time making small talk with this man. He had already decided that this boat would be ideal for crossing the Channel to France.

'Of course, it would be a pleasure.' Richard smiled.

'Well, she certainly looks in good condition. How old is

she?' Maxwell stood surveying the decks and the equipment. There was a dinghy with an outboard motor strapped to the stern. 'That might come in handy,' he thought.

Richard led Maxwell into the wheelhouse. He took a bunch of keys from his jacket and proceeded to start the motor. 'There you are, first time, she always runs like clockwork, not bad for 20 years old, don't you think?'

He went outside and began to undo the ropes attached to the mooring ring.

'Right, here we go, so many boats tied up here, you do have to be careful as you make your way out of the Marina to avoid any collisions.

He sat down on the seat in front of the steering wheel and concentrated on sailing the boat safely, until they were out at sea.

'Let us get into deeper water then I can get some speed up, I expect you would like to see how fast she can sail?' Richard was obviously enjoying himself.

Maxwell stood watching every move, how Richard steered the boat, and what speed had they now achieved.

'How many miles do you get from a tank of diesel?' Maxwell thought it would be helpful to know how far he would be able to sail without running out of fuel.

'I usually fill up the tank if I am going on a long journey. We are lucky to have a Fuel Berth at the Marina, which is very handy. She runs on low Sulphur Diesel. I have never run out of fuel. I did fill her up a week ago so there is plenty of fuel at the moment.

To be honest, I have never kept a log on how many miles she does on a full tank. Would you like to have a go at steering her for a while?'

'Yes, thank you, I would like that very much.' Maxwell was only too happy to take over the wheel. He sat looking at all the different dials.

'Well, this is fun. Time to talk money. How much were you thinking of asking?' Maxwell had already made his mind up. This was just what he was looking for.

'Considering her age, I am prepared to let her go for £30,000. I think that is a fair price. You would have to pay a great deal more if you were buying her from a dealer.'

'I agree with you. It will be a cash transaction of course. No messing about with banks.

When you are not moored at the Marina, what do you have to do if you want to moor out at sea?' Maxwell wanted to bring this conversation to an end.

'I suppose you throw down the anchor. You had better show me what to do. How do I turn off the engine?'

Richard showed him what to do. 'Come outside and I will take you through the drill on how to moor her.' Richard turned and headed for the rail.

Maxwell grabbed the Fire Extinguisher, which was hanging next to the steering wheel and as Richard bent over the rail, Maxwell brought down the heavy metal on his head with a mighty thud and pushed Richard over the side of the boat.

Maxwell stood looking at the body floating head down in the water. He was not sure whether the blow to Richard's head had killed him, but he would soon drown in that position he thought.

'Well, that's saved me £30,000.' He smiled to himself. 'Silly man, you were told it was bad luck to change the name of the boat.' He laughed.

He walked back to the wheelhouse and hung the fire extinguisher back on the hook by the steering wheel and restarted the engine. 'You were right, starts first time, she'll be taking me to France in no time.'

'However, I have something to do first. I better decide where to moor her and make my way back to the van. It is only 2pm, plenty of time for what I want to do next.' Maxwell smiled to himself.

'Just a minute, why don't I sail back to the Marina. If

anyone questions me, I can say that Mr. Burrows is going away for the weekend, and he has given me permission to try out the boat.

I can say that we have already agreed the price and that I want to show the boat to my wife and little girl. I can't buy it without my wife's permission, can I?'

He sat down at the steering wheel again and managed to turn the boat in the direction they had come.

'I don't suppose they will find the body for several days. It will probably sink. It will give me time to see whether Laura is living at the bungalow that belonged to her aunt. If she's not there I will have to sail to France on my own.'

CHAPTER FORTY-SIX

Maxwell managed to moor the boat and luckily no one approached him to ask where Mr. Richard Burrows was.

He quickly made his way back to the van and looked at the map again to remind himself where the bungalow was. He soon reached his destination.

He parked the van facing up the road and slid over into the passenger seat. He opened the window and began to move the mirror into position until he could see the driveway of the bungalow. There were no cars parked there at the moment.

He sat thinking what to do next. 'Do I take a chance and go over there, perhaps I can get to the back of the bungalow and look through the windows? I could be sitting here for hours and never see anyone.'

He climbed back onto the driver's seat and opened the door. He climbed down, locking the door of the van after him. He made his way across the road and walked up to the front door.

'I could just ring the bell, if the aunt answers, she won't know who I am and I can make some excuse why I'm here.'

He decided to ring the bell and stood there waiting for someone to answer the door. As no one came, he thought he would try the side gate and as it was unlocked, he walked straight through to the back garden.

He stood peering in the windows, but the net curtains were blocking his view. He tried the back door but that was locked.

He stood thinking how he could open it. There was a window next to the door. He looked around the garden and saw a small shed. Maybe there was something that he could use to prize the window open.

He went inside the shed, there were tools hanging on hooks, he chose a screwdriver and made his way back to the door.

After a few attempts to prize the window open, it gave way, and he was able to put his arm inside. Luckily, the key was in the lock. He managed to stretch across and open the door.

He stood looking around. Not much to see in the kitchen so he thought he would look in the bedrooms. He immediately saw something that made him stand still.

On one of the single beds, there was Mia's favourite toy, Bunny. There was no mistaking it, one of the ears was drooping down and the other ear was standing up.

'Got you Laura, so this is where you have been hiding all these months.' He felt like tearing the place to shreds but if he was going to trap Laura and Mia into coming with him to the Marina, he had to have a plan.

He quickly put the key back in the lock of the back door and pulled down the side window. He didn't want anyone to realize that he had been here.

'I had better go and sit in the van and wait for them to come home. Perhaps Mia is at playschool, she might be home by about 4pm.

Maybe, Laura has got herself a job, after all she didn't have any money when she left, I made sure of that.' He quickly made his way out into the garden, replaced the screwdriver into the shed and walked down the side of the bungalow shutting the side gate.

He crossed over the road back to the van and let himself in. He sat in the passenger seat where he had a good view through the mirror, of the driveway.

He looked at his watch, it was 3.30pm, maybe he wouldn't have too long to wait.

About half an hour later, a small white car arrived and parked on the drive. Maxwell was watching intently. A woman got out of the driving seat and turned to open the back door. 'That's not Laura, that woman has brown hair, Laura is blonde.'

But as he stared at her, she reached in and lifted a little girl from her car seat. Maxwell got a good look at her face. 'It is Laura, she has obviously dyed her hair brown.'

Maxwell had to stop himself from flinging the van door open and running across the road. He managed to resist the temptation. 'Now is not the right time.' He was breathing hard and clenching his fists.

'I will have to plan something for tomorrow. Laura and Mia are coming with me, whether they like it or not.'

He watched the two of them let themselves in the front door. 'I think I will wait around for a bit longer to see who else is living in the bungalow. Maybe Laura has got herself a boyfriend?

You're going to regret what you've done Laura.' Maxwell sat glowering at the bungalow.

He sat looking in the mirror for another hour and was just about ready to give up and make his way back to the

Bed and Breakfast Hotel, when another car, stopped and parked on the drive.

Another woman got out and went to the boot and got out some shopping bags.

Maxwell recognized her. It was Laura's sister Jacky! 'I should have known that it would be her hiding Laura. She made it clear at the wedding that she was against me marrying Laura.

I'll just wait for another half an hour to see if anyone else arrives, then I'll go back to the B&B. There might be a boyfriend. Laura might have decided to leave me because she had fallen for someone else.'

About three quarters of an hour later, another car pulled up and parked at the bottom of the drive.

Maxwell stared through the mirror, waiting to see who would open the car door. Adam got out and walked to the back of the car and opened the boot. He had stopped on the way to do some shopping.

Maxwell got a good look at him. 'I wonder who this is? Is he Jacky's boyfriend or Laura's?'

The front door opened, and Maxwell soon got his answer. Laura came running out and threw her arms around Adam. They both hugged each other and then walked into the bungalow.

'Well Laura, so that's why you ran away. I wonder how long it has been going on. What a shame you won't ever see him again after tomorrow. I'm going to make you suffer, you can be sure of that.'

Maxwell decided to make his way back to the hotel. He bought some fish and chips and sat in the van and ate them. He suddenly felt very hungry.

There would be plenty to do tomorrow. He would have to be up early so he could get back to the bungalow and hopefully follow Laura to Mia's playschool.

He had a plan to get Laura and Mia to the Marina and then make his way out to sea and head for France. He smiled to himself, it had been a very productive day, he now had a boat and he had found where Laura was staying, not bad for a few hours work.

CHAPTER FORTY-SEVEN

It had been a hot sunny day yesterday, and the mist was rising from the water. There had been a high tide at 3am this morning but it was now receding, leaving the beach washed clean.

A man was out walking his dog, enjoying the peace and quiet, taking deep breaths of the fresh morning air. He loved this time of day, an early walk on the beach, before the rest of the world was awake.

Suddenly his dog seemed agitated, pulling on his lead. 'What's the matter with you Jasper. What have you seen?'

The man unclipped the lead from his collar and the dog ran off at speed along the beach. Suddenly he stopped and began to bark at something.

'What have you found, you silly old dog?' The man

began to run to the spot where the dog was standing.

There on the beach was the body of a man, face down with his arms spread out, looking as if he had been swimming. He was fully clothed except that one of his shoes was missing.

The man got hold of his dog and clipped him back on his lead. He stood for a few minutes silently looking at the body, not knowing what to do.

'Should I touch him, perhaps not after all there is nothing I can do for the poor man, he's obviously dead.'

He took out his mobile phone and dialed 999. A voice answered. 'Police, Ambulance or Fire Brigade?'

'I think I need the Police and an Ambulance. There is a dead body on the beach, I was walking my dog and he found him. Someone needs to get here as soon as possible.'

The man gave directions on how to reach the spot and then he sat down and put his arms around his dog and waited for someone to arrive.

It did not take long before he heard the sirens of the Police and Ambulance arriving and suddenly there seemed to be people everywhere.

'Did you touch the body Sir?' a Policeman asked.

'No, I knew he was dead and that you would want me to leave the body as I found it, just in case there were any clues as to what had happened. Poor devil, I wonder how long he had been in the water?'

'Not long by the looks of him, maybe a day or two? I gather you have no idea who he is?'

'I've never seen him before in my life and never want to see him again. I'm feeling rather shaky, it's not something you see every day when you're out taking the dog for a walk.' The man sat with his head bowed.

The Police erected a tent around the dead body but of course they would soon have to let the Ambulance crew take the body to hospital. He could not be left on the shoreline, as the tide would soon be coming in again.

The Police took the man's name and address, who found the body, and said they would be in touch later that day in case he remembered anything that could be of help.

The man was grateful when they said he could go home. He wanted to tell his wife what had happened this morning.

He was not sure whether he would be taking Jasper for his early morning walks along the beach ever again.

He was finding it hard to get the sight of the dead body out of his mind. Perhaps the park would be a safer option from now on.

CHAPTER FORTY-EIGHT

The body on the beach had been taken to the local hospital. He was carefully undressed and examined for injuries.

He did have a large lump on the top of his head but apart from that there was no other explanation why this man had been found dead on the beach.

His clothes were examined and luckily in the top pocket of his jacket, there was a wallet which had not suffered too much trauma in the sea.

Inside there was some money, a bus pass with a photograph on the front and a picture of presumably, his wife, standing on the deck of a Cabin Cruiser.

They now had his name, Richard Burrows, and would immediately be able to set about finding his relatives and telling them the sad news of his demise.

Hopefully, after more examinations, they would be able to ascertain why this poor man was found on the beach this morning, dead.

Two Police Officers were sent to the address on the bus pass but after ringing the doorbell several times, there seemed to be no one home. They then knocked on the house next door to try to get information about Mr. Burrows.

The next-door neighbour was very shocked to hear about the death of her good friend. She was able to tell the police that his wife had died about six months ago and she knew of no other relatives.

The Police asked whether she thought that Mr. Burrows had been suffering from depression and might have thought of taking his own life but was assured that he seemed to be coping as well as could be expected with the loss of his beloved wife.

They asked if he had any hobbies to keep him busy and she told them that he had a boat moored at the Marina and went there most days just to keep the boat in good condition and meet up with friends.

He did say some weeks ago that he was thinking of selling it, but she said that he had put the boat up for sale, but as yet, had no offers.

The Police officers said they would keep her informed as to when the body would be released after all the examinations had been finalized and a death certificate showing the cause of death.

Unfortunately, this would sadly take some time and maybe she would be kind enough to let any of his friends and family know what had happened.

Obviously, his neighbour was extremely upset. She had lived next door to Mr. Burrows for years and the thought of him drowning in the sea was very distressing.

She said she knew he was a good sailor and that he had never had any accidents, such as falling overboard. Had the Police any clues as to what had happened?'

They replied that it would take some time to try and find the cause of death. At the moment, he did not appear to have drowned.

The Police Officers offered her their condolences and gave her their card with telephone numbers on it. If she had any information that might be helpful, would she please call them.

CHAPTER FORTY-NINE

Maxwell drove the van back to the B&B and on entering he stopped at the Reception Desk.

'Could you please make up my bill for the morning. I have an early appointment so can I have my breakfast at 7am?'

'Certainly sir, that will be no trouble. I am always up and about at that time of day.' The receptionist smiled at Maxwell.

Maxwell climbed the stairs to his room. He was quite happy to be leaving, hopefully he would be on his way to France tomorrow and if everything went well, he would have Laura and Mia with him.

He sat down on the bed and decided to look up on his laptop the best way to reach the English Channel sailing from the Marina. Once he reached the Channel, he hoped sailing across to France would be easy.

He decided to leave early in the morning and return to the bungalow where he would lie in wait for Laura when she left to take Mia to playschool.

He would follow at a safe distance and then he would know where to go in the afternoon and wait for Mia to come out. He would then make Laura come with him to the Marina.

He knew she would not want Mia to be frightened so it would be easy for Laura to pretend that they were just going on a little holiday. Maxwell smiled to himself, 'I was always going to find you Laura and now I have.'

Thank goodness this is the last night I am going to have to sleep in this hell hole. Once we are back in Greece, I will buy a lovely villa for us all to live in.

I wonder what happened to my father's Taverna? Perhaps one of my relatives is still working there?'

He switched off his laptop and made himself ready for bed. He lay there thinking what he would need tomorrow.

He would have to shop for some provisions. Who knows how long they would be on the boat?

He would let himself into the bungalow again and do some packing for Laura and Mia, after all they would need a change of clothes.

He finally fell sound asleep in the knowledge that everything was going just like clockwork, and he would soon be reunited with his daughter.

CHAPTER FIFTY

Maxwell had a restless night. His mind was full of the plans he had made for the morning.

He ate his breakfast, then showered and shaved. He packed his bags and made his way down to Reception. His bill was ready to be paid and he paid in cash.

The Receptionist said 'I hope you will be back to see us again Sir. I hope you have enjoyed your stay?'

Maxwell just nodded and left, putting his bags in the back of the van. He hoped he would be in good time to wait and see where Laura was taking Mia to playschool.

He soon arrived at the address of the bungalow and decided to face the way Laura would be leaving. If he parked the other way round, he might lose sight of her car while he was trying to turn the van around.

He would just have to duck his head down when she was putting Mia in the car seat and hope that she did not see him.

He was early and had a long wait before anyone stirred in the bungalow. The first person to leave was Jacky, Maxwell made sure he wasn't seen. She was obviously off to her hairdressing job.

About half an hour later, the front door opened, and Laura came out holding Mia's hand.

Laura unlocked the car and helped Mia into her car seat. She put a bag into the boot and then drove away.

Maxwell kept a safe distance as he followed her. After a short journey, Laura stopped the car, helped Mia out and walked hand in hand to the door of a wooden building. A lady greeted them at the entrance and smiled at Laura as Mia waved goodbye.

Maxwell wondered whether to follow Laura to where she was working but thought he would rather go back to the bungalow and collect some clothes for Laura and Mia and then take them to the boat.

He drove back to the bungalow and went to the side gate and into the back garden and took the screwdriver from the shed and prized open the kitchen window, then using the key, he opened the back door.

He went straight into the bedroom and took down a suitcase from the top of the wardrobe and opened the chest of drawers and the wardrobe and packed the suitcase full of clothes.

He was about to leave when he suddenly remembered to take Bunny from the bed and put him into the suitcase as well. He smiled to himself, he would soon have his little girl back, where she was supposed to be.

He carefully replaced the key in the back door and the screwdriver in the shed and made his way back to the van.

He stopped at a small grocery store and bought some food and drinks for the journey ahead, then made his way back to the Marina. It was still early in the morning, he hoped that no one would challenge him when he walked along the path and climbed onboard the Cabin Cruiser. Luckily no one saw Maxwell, he was quick to go below, and begin putting away the food and drinks he had bought.

There was a small wardrobe in the double cabin, and he unpacked the case and hung up some of the clothes he had taken from the bungalow.

He sat down at the little table in the galley and felt pleased with himself that everything had gone to plan.

All he had to do now was wait until it was time to drive back to the Playschool and wait for Laura to appear to pick up Mia. He was looking forward to that.

He decided to have a sleep, he was rather tired with all the stress of keeping tracks on Laura and so he lay down on the double bed and tried to empty his head about the problems of the last two days.

He had the boat and would soon have Mia. His plans were working out and soon he would be sailing across the English Channel to France. At last, he managed to fall asleep.

CHAPTER FIFTY-ONE

Maxwell woke with a start. He lay there thinking how he was going to leave the Marina. He was planning to sail out as soon as it was dusk.

He was going to keep a low profile on the boat. He decided to keep below deck, he did not want to get into any conversations with the people in the next mooring bays.

Obviously when he brought back Laura and Mia to the Marina, he might have to make up some excuse why he was there without Mr. Burrows.

Maybe, he could say that Mr. Burrows had gone away for a few days and that he had said Maxwell could show the boat to his wife and daughter.

Maxwell could say that he had bought the boat and was just waiting to finalize the paperwork. Yes, that seemed reasonable enough, however, hopefully he would not have to explain why he was there on his own.

It was now 2.30pm, he had slept for hours. He decided to make his way back to the playschool where Laura had taken Mia this morning.

He was about to leave, when he smiled to himself and found a plastic bag. He bungled Bunny into it and made his way back on deck. He looked cautiously around him and then quickly made his way out of the Marina and back to his van.

He drove the short distance to the playschool and parked where he could see Laura arriving. There was plenty of time for him to decide what he was going to say to her, and he was looking forward to seeing her face when she realized he had found her.

Soon it was 3.30pm and mothers and fathers were arriving to pick up their children. Maxwell was watching intently for Laura to appear. He did not have long to wait.

When she stood watching for Mia to come out, he crept up behind her.

'Hello Laura, you didn't expect to see me here, did you?'

CHAPTER FIFTY-TWO

Laura stood still, hardly able to breath, she thought she was going to faint.

She knew that voice only too well. She sometimes had nightmares about Maxwell finding her and would wake up in a cold sweat. Now the nightmare had come true.

Before she had the chance to turn and speak to him, Mia came running up to her. She suddenly stopped and was looking at the man beside Laura. He seemed familiar but there was something different about him.

Suddenly she cried 'Daddy' and ran into his arms. Maxwell picked her up and hugged her.

'Hello, my little Princess, didn't you recognize your father?'

'You haven't got your beard Daddy, what have you done

with it? I liked it because it tickled when you kissed me. Why haven't you been to visit us before?'

'I've been very busy with work but now we can go on a lovely long holiday, that will be lovely won't it. Look who I have brought to come on holiday with us?' Maxwell pulled out Bunny from his bag and gave it to Mia.

'Where did you get that from?' Laura finally managed to speak. 'Have you been in the bungalow, how did you get inside?'

Maxwell just laughed, 'I also packed a suitcase for you both. You are coming with me on a little holiday.'

'I don't think so Maxwell, I know what you have done, and Mia and I are going nowhere with you.' Laura whispered. She didn't want to frighten Mia.

'Well, my daughter is coming with me, you don't have to come but I think it would be best if you do.'

'Mummy, why don't you want to come on holiday with Daddy and me?'

'It's just that Mummy has a job doesn't she, and I don't know if they will let me have time off to go on holiday. We can go some other time, can't we?'

Maxwell smiled at Mia. 'Mummy is being silly. I have already asked her boss if she can have some time off and he said yes.'

He looked at Laura. 'You will enjoy yourself when you see how we are going to travel. I have made some arrangements and it will be fun, won't it Mia?'

'Well, I had better ring Jacky at work, if we don't come home this evening, she will be on to the Police to find us.' Laura looked him straight in the eyes.

'Very well, you can ring Jacky, but I will be listening to everything you say, so you better be careful.' Laura dialed Jacky's number at work.

'Hello Laura, are you OK?' Jacky sounded worried.

'Yes, I'm just ringing to tell you that Mia has been invited to a Birthday Party. You know that little girl that I told you Mia was friends with, Rebecca, well we are going to her house straight from playschool.'

'He's there isn't he, oh my god.'

'Yes, so we won't want any tea, so you go ahead and have yours, See you later.' Laura signed off.

'Right, you won't be needing your phone where we are going, so you might as well give it to me.' Maxwell took it from her hand.

'Let's get going then, we haven't got far to go until I can show you the surprise that I have waiting for you both.'

Maxwell picked up Mia and began to walk towards his van. Laura had no alternative but to follow him.

CHAPTER FIFTY-THREE

Maxwell put Laura and Mia in the back of the van, telling them he was taking them to the surprise, and that he did not want them to know where they were going.

He soon arrived at the Marina and parked a short distance from the entrance. He went to the back of the van and unlocked it.

He lifted down Mia and carried her close to his chest. Laura had no alternative but to follow him. Maxwell walked down the pathway until he came to the 'Christina.'

'Well, what do you think of her? I have bought her so we can go sailing. That will be fun Mia, our very own boat to go just where we want to?'

'Do you know how to sail Daddy? I have never been on a boat before. It's going to be very exciting.' Mia smiled at

Maxwell.

Laura stood beside them, wondering what Maxwell was planning. 'Where was he going to sail to? Did he know how to sail?'

She noticed that there was a 'For Sale' notice attached to a post beside the boat. Who had he bought this boat from?'

'Well, don't let us just stand here, let us get on board and then I can show you around.' They were just about to climb on deck, when a man suddenly approached Maxwell.

'Excuse me sir, but I believe I saw you yesterday with Mr. Richard Burrows. Have you bought his boat?'

'Yes, I have. I paid cash for it yesterday. There is still some paperwork to be signed but Mr. Burrows said as he was going away for the weekend, he did not mind if I showed the boat to my wife and daughter. It was a lovely surprise for them, I've only just told them that it is ours and they can't wait to see on board.'

'Well, I'm sure they are going to have some wonderful adventures. If there are any questions about the boat, I will be only too happy to help you in any way I can?

I am moored just down the way. My name is Peter Jackson, it was very nice to meet you and your family. I hope you will all enjoy being part of the sailing community. You didn't say what your name was?'

'Just let me help my wife and daughter on board, they are so excited to see what I have bought, they can't wait to look around.'

He lifted Mia and helped Laura step onto the deck. 'You two go below and see the cabins. I won't be a moment.'

He turned back to Peter Jackson. 'My name is David Turner, but you can call me Dave. I look forward to being friends.

I am sure I will need to ask you all sorts of questions about the boat in the future. It is a very long time since I did any sailing. I'm a bit rusty but can't wait to get out on the sea again.

It was very nice to meet you, hope to see you again very soon.' Maxwell shook his hand and stepped onto the deck.

He was in a hurry to see what Laura and Mia were doing, they had disappeared down below.

Laura was sitting on the bench in the galley and Mia was looking in the cabins.

'What do you think you are doing Maxwell. Do you even know how to sail a boat? Since when did you have any lessons?

Where are you thinking of taking us? You could be putting Mia's life in danger. It is treacherous out there on the ocean.'

Laura was not afraid of Maxwell anymore. The time away from him, had made her realize that he had no hold over her. Why had she let him bully her for all those years, she wondered?

'I know the Police are after you and it will not be long until they find you. Why don't you do the sensible thing and let Mia and me go?

This is only going to make things worse for you when they do catch up with you.' Laura got up and followed Mia into the larger cabin to see what she was doing.

Suddenly the bedroom door slammed behind her, she heard the key turn. Maxwell had locked them in.

Obviously, he had no intention of letting them go.

CHAPTER FIFTY-FOUR

'Adam, I've just had a telephone call from Laura. She said she was going to a birthday party from playschool at Rebecca's house. That secret word means Maxwell has found her.

I'm in a terrible state, I don't know what to do?' Jacky began to cry.

'Oh, my God, how did he find her? We have got to tell the police. There is no way we will be able to find her on our own.' Adam was horrified that Maxwell had Laura and Mia. What was he going to do with them?

'Jacky, go home to the bungalow and I will get there as fast as I can. Have you any photographs of Laura and Mia together. We will need to take them to the Police Station, so they will know who they are looking for.'

'Thank you, Adam. I think I know where there are some photos. Please get here as quickly as you can.'

Adam was soon on his way. This was the nightmare that he had hoped would never happen. Maxwell was a murderer. Who knows what he might do? He was obviously desperate. Why had he taken them, perhaps he intended to use Laura and Mia as hostages?

'We should have gone to the police before now, maybe they would have been able to keep Laura and Mia safe, just in-case Maxwell turned up?'

When Adam arrived at the bungalow, Jacky had obviously been keeping watch for him.

'I'm so glad you are here. I have managed to find some photographs. Come in and look at them and we can decide which would be best to take to the Police Station?' Jacky led him inside.

'Please God, don't let him hurt them, I couldn't bare it?' Jacky began to cry.

'The sooner we get to the Police station and tell them Laura's story, they will be able to start searching for them. Let's have a look at the photographs.' Adam sat down and began to look through the pictures.

'This one of them both is beautiful. It is so clear. I am sure the Police will be able to use it.

Do you know where the nearest Police Station is?'

'No, I have never had reason to go there before. Let us look it up on-line.' Jacky turned on her laptop. They soon found the address and decided to go in Adam's car.

On the way, they discussed the right way to explain why Laura had run away, and had not told the Police before now, where she was hiding.

'I'm sure they will understand why she hasn't come forward. She knew nothing about his first wife, except that he told her she had run away with her boyfriend. There was no reason why Laura would know otherwise.'

They soon reached the Police Station. They entered and walked up to the Reception Desk.

'How can I help you sir?' The policeman on duty asked.

'We would like to talk to someone about Maxwell Hudson. He is the husband of my sister Laura and I believe he has kidnapped her and her daughter Mia.'

'Right, would you both like to take a seat and I will find out who is available to see you?'

The Policeman dialed a number and spoke to someone. 'A Detective is coming to take you to his office. He will be here shortly.'

Jacky grabbed Adam's hand. 'Do you think they will be able to find them?'

'I don't know but I can't think of anything else we can do. He could be anywhere?'

A Detective arrived and ushered them into his office.

'What can I do for you? I believe you have some information concerning Maxwell Hudson?'

'My sister Laura is married to Maxwell and a few months ago she ran away from him taking her daughter Mia with her because of his controlling behaviour.

He would not let her have any friends, she was forbidden to ring me, her sister. He put a tracker on her car so that he knew exactly where she was.

There were so many horrible things that he did that she decided she could no longer bear to live with him.

Our Aunt died recently and left her bungalow to me and my sister, so I wrote and told her. At last, she had somewhere to come to and she has been hiding from him for the past six months.'

'Why have you decided to come here today and tell me this?' The Detective wrote something in his notebook.

'Obviously we saw on the news that the body in the garden of the house that Maxwell owned, was his first wife and that he was on the run. We hoped you would be able to arrest him and then Laura would be safe to come out of hiding.

I had a telephone call at 3.45pm from my sister. We had arranged that if Maxwell found her, she would ring me and use the name 'Rebecca' in a sentence, which would mean that Maxwell was there.

I am terrified what he might do to them. My sister had just picked up her daughter Mia from playschool, so he must have been waiting there for them both.' Jacky began to cry.

'If you would excuse me, I need to talk to one of my colleagues, I am not up to date as to where we are, concerning Maxwell Hudson. Hopefully, it will not take too long to get some recent information.' The Detective left the room.

'What do you think Adam. Will they be able to find them both?'

'Well, I suppose they will have a better chance than we have. Where would we look?

Just a minute, I have just remembered something. When I came down last night there was a white van parked across the road.

I decided to take down the registration number. It was still there when I left to go home.

I'm not really sure why I did it. I had never seen it before, but something made me wonder what it was doing there at that time of night.

I wish I had walked across the road and looked inside to see who was there. It is possible it was Maxwell watching the bungalow?'

'Perhaps it was Maxwell, I think you should tell the Detective when he comes back. Maybe if they can find the van, Laura and Mia might be hidden in it?' Jacky was trying to be positive.

The door opened and two Detectives entered the room. 'Perhaps you would like to start from the beginning and then we might be able to decide what is the best course of action to find your sister and her daughter.'

Adam quickly explained that he had taken the registration number of the white van that was parked across the road from the bungalow. 'Maybe if you could find the van, it might lead you to Maxwell. It's worth trying, sadly we have no idea where he might have taken them both.'

'I think the best idea is that you both return home and wait and see if Maxwell rings you and makes any demands.

We will do everything we can to try and find where he has taken them.' The Detectives rose and shook their hands and walked with them to the entrance.

CHAPTER FIFTY-FIVE

'Jacky, I just can't go back to the bungalow and sit still waiting for someone to ring us. I'll go mad. I must do something to try and find Laura and Mia.

I keep thinking, why didn't I go across the road, and look in the van to see who was sitting there. Maybe if I had and it was Maxwell, I could have at least phoned the police.'

'Adam, you can't blame yourself, no-one thought Maxwell had found out where Laura was living. How on earth did he work out where she was?' Jacky sighed.

'I'll drive you home and you can sit by the phone, in case the Police ring. I'm going to drive around looking for the white van. Thank goodness I wrote down the registration number.'

'Please be careful Adam. We now know that Maxwell is

a murderer. Who knows what he is capable of?

The only thing I am clinging to, is that Maxwell does love his daughter, I'm sure he won't want to harm her.' Jacky began to cry again.

'Let's try to look on the positive, perhaps he has taken Laura and Mia somewhere safe and wants to use them as hostages for his freedom.' Adam took a deep breath. He wasn't sure whether to hope that was what Maxwell had taken them for, all he wanted was them to be safe.

'Right Jacky, here we are, you go and wait by the telephone and if someone rings you with good news that they have been found then please immediately ring me.'

Adam let her out of the car. 'Right, I'm going to drive around the streets to see if I can find the van, I've wasted enough time already, take care of yourself, I'm sure the police will find them soon.

By the way, don't open the door, if you don't know who it is, well wish me luck.'

Adam immediately started his car and began to drive slowly around the neighbouring roads, stopping and looking up and down them.

He was beginning to feel tired and wondered if he was on a wild goose chase. He had been driving for some time, when he saw a sign for the Marina.

He drove down the road and parked near the entrance, and there it was, the white van.

He sat still for a few moments, hardly able to believe his luck. He parked the car a short distance from the back of the van and locked his car.

He walked slowly down to the van and crept along the side windows and peered in. No one was sitting there. He wondered what to do next.

He rang Jacky. 'Hello, I've just found the white van, it's parked near the Marina. No one is in it, but I think I will walk into the Marina and see if I can find out who it belongs to. At least we might be able to eliminate it from Maxwell using it to hide across the road.

Perhaps you should ring the Police and tell them I have found the van and maybe they will want to come and see if they can open the rear door. There might be some indication of what the van was carrying.'

'Please be careful Adam, who knows what Maxwell will do if you find him. No one has rung me. I haven't left the phone for a moment, just in case someone does.'

'I've got one of the photos of Laura and Mia with me. I suppose if I see anyone in the Marina, I could ask them if they had seen a lady with a little girl.' Adam said.

'Anyway, it is beginning to get dark, I had better hurry

up and look around the place, maybe Maxwell could be hiding them here. I'll talk to you again soon.'

Adam made his way around the Marina, most of the boats did not seem to have anyone on board to ask whether they had seen a lady and little girl.

Just as Adam was about to give up hope. A gentleman who was standing on the deck of a cabin cruiser called out, 'Can I help you? You look as if you are lost. Just a moment, I'll come down and bring a torch.'

Adam waited until the gentleman descended from his boat. 'Are you looking for a particular boat, do you know the name?'

'No, I'm afraid I don't. Actually, I'm looking for a young lady and her daughter.

I've got a photo of them here perhaps you would be kind enough to look at it and tell me whether you have seen them?' Adam took the photo from his wallet and the man shone his torch so that he could see it properly.

'Yes, I saw this lady and her little girl this afternoon, her husband had just bought a boat from Mr. Richard Burrows. He said that Mr. Burrows had told him he could show his wife and daughter around the boat.

His name was, let me think, that's right, it was Dave Turner. He said he had paid cash for the boat but still had papers to be signed.

Would you like me to show you where the boat is berthed, it's not very far away?'

'Yes please, I need to have a talk with them about some sad news.' Adam didn't want this gentleman to spook Maxwell into doing something to Laura or Mia.

'Right, here we go, it's not that far, sorry to hear you are the bearer of bad news. What a shame when they were so happy.' Peter Jackson led the way.

The light was fading and soon they reached the berth where the 'Christina' was supposed to be docked. 'Oh, that's strange, surely Mr. Turner hasn't taken the boat out to sea. He should have waited until all the paperwork was signed.

I think that Richard just wanted him to have a look around. This isn't good. I don't think that Mr. Turner had sailed a boat for years. They could get into trouble.'

Adam was horrified. 'What was Maxwell thinking? Was he making a break for freedom by sailing the boat somewhere he could escape to?'

'What do you think we should do, should we report the boat to the authorities to look out for them. I would hate anything to happen to his wife and daughter.

Perhaps we should contact the RNLI to come out on

patrol or the Coastguard to look for them. He is a very foolish man, taking such a risk. I wish I had known what he had planned to do.' Mr. Jackson was looking really worried.

'I might as well tell you the truth, the man who spoke to you today is in fact Maxwell Hudson, who is wanted by the Police for the murder of his first wife.

The lady and little girl that you saw, ran away from him about six months ago because of his coercive behaviour.

How he has managed to find her, we don't know?'

'Oh, good gracious, obviously I had no idea. We had better call the Police. I feel dreadful, but he knew the boat belonged to Mr. Richard Burrows and he obviously had the keys. Perhaps he had somehow stolen them from him?'

Adam rang the number on the card that the Detective had given him. 'It is Adam Marsh here, I have found the white van that was parked near Laura's bungalow, it is on a side street near the Marina. I have been walking around to see if I could find Laura and Mia.

A gentleman on one of the boats asked me who I was looking for and I showed him a photo of them.

He said that they were with a gentleman called Dave Turner, but of course it was Maxwell Hudson. He said he had bought a boat named the 'Christina' from Mr. Richard Burrows.'

The Detective said 'Let me stop you there. Did you say a Mr. Richard Burrows owned the boat called the 'Christina?'

A man's body was found on the beach yesterday morning and has now been identified as Mr. Richard Burrows.

We were coming to the Marina tomorrow to see if anyone had any information as to why this gentleman was found dead. His neighbour said he had a boat named after his wife called the 'Christina.'

'Oh my god.' Peter Jackson who had been listening to the conversation with the Detective was shaking his head. 'Surely this man, Maxwell, hasn't killed Richard?'

Adam was just as horrified, 'Maxwell has taken the 'Christina' and has sailed out to sea with Laura and Mia on board.

Please could you get in touch with the Coastguard or some-one to look out for the boat. Anything could happen to them?'

The Detective said he would ask for a search to be made for the 'Christina' and that he and a colleague would be at the Marina as soon as possible.

Also, he would arrange for the radio to put out information about Maxwell Hudson who is already wanted for the murder of his first wife and now was wanted for questioning, concerning the body found on the beach yesterday morning.

It had been identified as Mr. Richard Burrows. Maxwell Hudson has stolen the cabin cruiser called 'Christina' which belonged to Mr. Burrows.

Also on board, are Laura Hudson and her daughter Mia, who have been abducted.

'Excuse me I must ring Laura's sister. She is sitting by the phone at home waiting for any news.' Adam rang Jacky.

'Jacky, I am at the Marina, there is a gentleman here who saw Laura and Mia this afternoon.

Maxwell was calling himself by a different name and said he had bought a boat. Unfortunately, the boat isn't here now, and we think that Maxwell has sailed out to sea. We have been in touch with the Police and hopefully someone will be out looking for it.'

'Adam, they could be anywhere, what my poor sister must be going through, she must be terrified what will happen to her and Mia.' Jacky was crying again.

'The Police are on their way here and they are putting out a call on the Radio asking for anyone who has seen the 'Christina', that's name of the boat, to let the Coastguard or the Police to know its whereabouts.

Please don't upset yourself, at least we now know,

Maxwell has them onboard, hopefully it won't be long before Laura and Mia can be rescued.'

'Please keep me informed of what is happening Adam. I am going out of my mind with worry.' Jacky pleaded.

'As soon as I know if the boat has been found and that Laura and Mia are safe, I will ring you.' Adam hoped he would have good news to report soon.

CHAPTER FIFTY-SIX

Maxwell had waited until the light had begun to fade and then decided it was time to leave the Marina. He told Laura and Mia to go down below. 'Why don't you make Mia something to eat, she must be hungry by now. I bought plenty of groceries, we might be at sea for quite a while.

Stay down below until I tell you it is safe to come back on deck. I need to concentrate on sailing the boat out of the Marina.'

'Where are you taking us Maxwell? Why don't you just let us go? I know you are wanted by the Police. You will just be getting into more trouble by keeping us here.'

'I never told you that I was born in Greece did I, well now I have decided I want to go back to my Homeland. Mia will have a good life there, she will learn to speak the language, and be brought up in the Greek culture where women know their place.

You never understood that did you Laura? I was trying to instill in you that a husband must be obeyed but no, you had to run away. You had a wonderful life, wanted for nothing, why couldn't you be satisfied with that?' Maxwell glared at her.

'In a marriage, neither person should have total control over the other. Ours was not a marriage, it was more like a prison sentence.

Perhaps if you had let me see my friends and I had some sort of life outside the home and was treated as an equal, maybe we could have been happy, but you were obviously unable to see that.'

'I saw you with your boyfriend outside the bungalow last night when you were hugging him. How long had that been going on before you decided to run away?'

'I didn't meet Adam before I left. I ran away because I found out what you were doing to those houses you bought.

You didn't refurbish them, you just painted over the filth and the poor people who were renting them were too scared of you to do anything about it. They obviously couldn't afford anything better, so they no choice but to live in those hovels.

When that poor lady turned up at our house, with her son, who was obviously very ill, and told me of the disgusting conditions they were living in, it was the final crack in our marriage.

It was then I found the courage to leave you. I wasn't going to live the rest of my life with a monster.'

Maxwell raised his arm to strike her, but then Mia, who had been asleep in the single cabin, climbed up the steps onto the deck.

'Why are you and Daddy shouting at each other.' Mia stood rubbing her eyes.

'Mummy is going down to the galley to make us something to eat. Why don't you come and see what goodies Daddy has bought us?' Laura took Mia by her hand and led her back down the stairs.

Maxwell started to look around and saw there was a VHF radio on the ledge by the window in the wheelhouse. He began to fiddle around with the dial until he had good reception.

He began to listen. Suddenly a broadcast by the Police interrupted the program.

'The dead body on the beach yesterday morning has been identified as Mr. Richard Burrows.

We believe that Mr. Burrows was murdered and his boat the 'Christina' has been stolen. Would anyone who has seen the boat, please get in contact with either with the Police or the Coastguard? This is an urgent message.'

Maxwell stood for a few minutes. They had sailed not far from the coast. Maxwell had been staying nearby deliberately, so he could find his way to the Channel.

'It won't be long before they catch up with us, the Coastguard or the RNLI have fast motors.

I'm like a sitting duck. I need to get off this boat and make a dash for the land and then find a way to get to France.'

He began to gather up the things he wanted to take with him. He would have to get his black holdall from the cabin, he would need the money to make his escape.

He picked up the VHF radio. 'I'll need this to keep track of where the coastguard or police are.'

He found a torch and opening a locker, discovered two adult size life jackets.

He went down the steps to the galley. Laura had made some sandwiches for Mia, and they were both sitting at the table.

'Do you want something to eat Maxwell?' Laura asked.

'Not now, although you could put some sandwiches in a

paper bag. I'll eat them later. I can't leave the wheelhouse for too long. I have got to steer the boat.'

He went into the double cabin and pulled out the black holdall containing the money.

His navy coat was hanging in the wardrobe, and he put it on. Looking around, he was trying to decide what else he should take with him.

He came back into the galley, 'What are you doing Maxwell? Why have you got that holdall?' Laura gave him the sandwiches that she had wrapped up.

'It's getting cold up on deck, I needed my coat.' Maxwell made his way back up the stairs.

Laura sat for a few minutes thinking. 'What was Maxwell up to?' She decided to follow him up the stairs onto the deck.

Laura couldn't believe her eyes. He was beginning to undo the cables that fastened the dinghy to the back of the boat. 'Surely, he was not going to leave her and Mia, stranded on the 'Christina' in the middle of the sea?'

Maxwell began to lower the dingy, with the cables still attached, down the side of the boat into the sea.

'Maxwell, what are you doing? I don't know how to sail this boat, what am I supposed to do?' Laura could not believe Maxwell could be this cruel.

'The Police are looking for the 'Christina.' It won't be long before someone finds me. I need to get away, if I stay here, I will end up in prison, is that what you want?'

'Frankly, yes, you've stolen this boat, haven't you? Don't you care what happens to your daughter?

I know what you did to your first wife. The police are going to catch up with you soon so you might as well give yourself up.'

Maxwell took one of the lifejackets from the locker and put it on. He grabbed his black holdall and without a second glance at Laura, he climbed down the boarding ladder into the dinghy.

He managed to start the outboard motor first time and he quickly disappeared from view, into the darkness.

Laura stood on the deck. She had no idea what to do next. Should she try to start the engine? Would it be best if she just let the boat drift along until somebody found them?

She looked in the locker where Maxwell had found the lifejacket, there was only one in there.

It was much too big for Mia, but it would have to do. There was a lifebuoy hanging on the railings, she would have to use that in an emergency.

She decided to go down to the galley. 'Mia, have you had enough to eat darling? There are some nice cakes, would you like one of them?' She didn't want to scare her although she was terrified herself.

'Yes, please Mummy.' Laura found an iced bun and gave it to her.

Laura thought 'I wonder what Maxwell did with my phone? He took it from me after I had rung Jacky. Obviously, Jacky knows that Maxwell has us. She would have contacted the police straight away.

They must be out looking for us. If I could just find the phone maybe there could be a signal out here, we are not far from the coast.'

Laura began to open the kitchen drawers and looked in the cupboards. She went into the cabin and searched the bedside cabinet.

Perhaps he had put it in the coat he was wearing when he took it from her. He was now wearing it as he sailed away, maybe with the phone still in his coat pocket.

'I wonder if he had hidden it in the wheelhouse. I won't be long Mia I just need to go up on deck and see if I can find something.'

It was becoming quite dark, how was she going to make sure that anyone searching for the 'Christina' would be able to see her.

In the wheelhouse, there was a lamp which appeared to

be full of paraffin, maybe she could light that and hang it somewhere it could be seen.

She remembered that there were matches in the kitchen. She hurriedly ran down the stairs to the galley. The matches were beside the stove. 'Won't be long darling, it is getting dark outside, and Mummy is going to light a lamp.'

She went back out on deck and managed to light the lamp but where to hang it?

She looked around her and decided to hang it on a hook in the Wheelhouse. Surely if someone saw a light in the window they would come and investigate why this boat wasn't moving?

If only she could find her mobile phone? The sea seemed to be rather choppy, surely there wasn't going to be a storm, as if she didn't have enough to contend with?'

She decided that they would have to attract the attention of any boat that might be sailing by them, and she began to look around in some of the boxes on deck.

One was painted with 'For Emergency Use.' She quickly opened it and looked inside. There were several objects. There was what looked like flares. Laura had seen these used on films but had no idea how to light them.

There was a box full of bandages, cotton wool and plasters, hopefully she would not need to use them, however she decided to take some cotton wool.

She quickly returned to the galley. 'Mia, we are going to play a game. You are going to dress up in a lifejacket and we are going to make lots of noise. We want to see if we can attract a boat to come and find us.

Daddy has gone in search of someone to help us as the boat has stopped working.

Come on let's go up on deck. I think we will take a couple of blankets to wrap ourselves in as it is getting rather cold.' Laura went into the cabin and took a couple of blankets off the bed.

'Let's take some saucepans and metal spoons and we can bang them as loud as we can. Someone on land might hear us and then they will get us some help.'

Laura helped Mia back on deck and took out the last lifejacket and put it on her.

'Don't you look wonderful. You look like a real sailor. Mummy hasn't got a lifejacket but there is a lifebuoy over on the railings if I need it. I've just noticed there is a whistle hanging from your jacket.

Mummy is going to take it and when we make a noise with the saucepans, Mummy is going to blow the whistle as hard as she can. We want to wake up someone in the houses on shore.

First of all I want you to put a little bit of cotton wool in your ears, I don't want your ears to hurt when we are making so much noise.'

Laura sat Mia on the box which said, 'For Emergency' and wrapped her in a blanket.

Laura then picked up the saucepan and metal spoon and gave it to Mia. 'Right let's start making a noise, bang the metal spoon on the saucepan as hard as you can.'

Laura began to bang two saucepan lids together and blew as hard as she could on the whistle.

They were facing the shore and Laura hoped that a house that was near the sea might hear the racket they were making and look out and see that they were in distress.

CHAPTER FIFTY-SEVEN

Adam was pacing up and down the path in the Marina. Where were the police, he had told them, he had found the white Van?

The Coastguard should be out looking for the 'Christina' by now. Maxwell couldn't have got that far away in the short time since he had sailed out of the Marina?

'I am so sorry, of course I didn't know what that man was up to. How could I? He had the keys to the boat and obviously knew Richard's name. Poor man, he loved his boat, he and his wife had such wonderful holidays on it.

It was very sad when she died. When he put the 'For Sale' notice up, I think he had decided that he didn't want to go sailing without her. When I think of the lady and the little girl, I hate to think what might happen to them.' Peter

Jackson was horrified.

'Please don't blame yourself. Here come the Detectives I saw earlier at the Police Station, hopefully they might have some good news?' Adam wished there was something else he could do.

'Hello, Mr. Adam Marsh, well done for finding the van. We have sent out a radio message for the public to look out for the 'Christina.' The Coastguard are already searching for her and hopefully we will have some good news soon.'

'They can't have got very far, I'm sure they only sailed out of the Marina as it was getting dark. I wonder where he is trying to reach, maybe the English Channel.

This is quite a busy stretch of water and now it is really dark you do have to be careful.'

Adam thought, thanks for saying that, as if I'm not worried enough already. 'Presumably, he is making his way down the coast, he wouldn't want to stray out to sea, he would need to follow the shoreline, wouldn't he?

Only an experienced sailor would want to be sailing in the dark, near a shipping lane?'

'Well, let's hope the Coastguard will soon find them, although it is rather worrying what Maxwell will do when they try and arrest him.' The Detective's phone rang.

'Apparently, someone who lives near the shore has

reported a boat that seems to be in distress. Someone on board is blowing a whistle and banging something to attract attention. It is not moving and there is only one small light.

The Coastguard are going to the position where the boat has been reported and let's hope it is the 'Christina.'

'Oh, I do hope so, I better ring Laura's sister Jacky and tell her we might have some good news soon. I wonder what Maxwell is doing, let's pray that he will let Laura and Mia go?'

CHAPTER FIFTY-EIGHT

'Mummy, I can't bang this saucepan anymore, my arms are too tired.' Mia sighed and looked at her mother.

'Don't worry darling, you have done a wonderful job. Let's wrap you up nice and warmly in this blanket and if you lie down on the big box maybe you can go to sleep for a little while.'

Laura was exhausted herself, but she knew she had to continue to make a noise. Surely someone would hear her. The boat hadn't moved, and she hoped that the houses near the shore would eventually wonder where the sound was coming from.

She continued to bang the saucepan with the steel spoon and blew the whistle until she thought she had no breath to continue. Just as she was about to give up, she saw a light go on in one of the houses on the shoreline.

Somehow Laura found some strength to continue to blow the whistle and bang the saucepan with all her might. Perhaps if she got the lamp from the wheelhouse, she could swing it back and forth so it might attract the attention of the people in the house.

She quickly retrieved the lamp and stood on the deck, waving it back and forth. She saw that another window had now got a light in it and near to tears she forced herself to keep going.

Suddenly, there was a bright light shining directly into her eyes. A voice called 'Ahoy there, are you Ok, we will be coming onboard.'

Laura nearly fell to her knees, she gently woke Mia, 'Darling wake up, someone has come to rescue us.'

'Who is onboard this boat. Is there a man called Maxwell Hudson?' The Coastguard was obviously being cautious.'

'There is only myself and my daughter, Maxwell took the dinghy and left us here. I didn't know how to sail the boat and I am so glad that you have found us.'

The Coastguard came onboard, Laura had never been so happy to see this gentleman who had come to rescue them.

'So, there is nothing wrong with the boat itself, it is just you were not sure how to sail it? Well, I am going to sail it for you back to the Marina, the Coastguard boat might continue to search for Maxwell Hudson. He might have left the dinghy somewhere and continued on foot to make his escape.'

'I think I will take Mia down to the cabin, she is exhausted and cold. Can I make you a hot drink or something? Laura felt like hugging him.

'No thank you, I'll be fine. The sooner we get you back to the Marina the better. Take the little girl down to the cabin and wrap her up warm.'

The Coastguard made his way to the wheelhouse. He turned the keys, and the engine came to life. He began to turn the boat in the right direction and soon was sailing back to the Marina.

Laura undid the life jacket that Mia was wearing and laid her down on the bed. 'Here's Bunny, he was wondering where you were. Try and go to sleep, a kind gentleman is taking us back where we came from, so we'll soon be back home.' Laura kissed her and tucked her in. 'You did really well Mia, I couldn't have done it without you.'

Laura went back on deck. 'How did you find us?'

A house on the shoreline heard you making a noise, and then saw the light being swung back and forth. The lady reported it to the Police, and they got in touch with us.'

'I wish I could thank that lady. We could have been in so much trouble.' Laura breathed a sigh of relief.

'Would you like to tell me something about Maxwell Hudson. I believe he was your husband?'

'Yes, unfortunately, he still is. I ran away about 6 months ago with my daughter. I don't know how he found me. I had seen on the television that he was wanted for the murder of his first wife. Of course, I knew nothing about that when I was married to him.

Now they think he must have murdered the gentleman whose boat this is. I hope they catch him soon. Maybe I shall have some peace when I know he is in custody.'

'Try not to worry, the good thing is, you and your daughter are safe now, that's all that matters.'

'You're quite right, I don't know what I would have done if you hadn't found us. I am so grateful.'

'Why don't you go down below and have a rest, you must be exhausted?'

'I think I will, are you sure there is nothing I can get you?'

'I'm fine it won't be long before we are back at the Marina.'

CHAPTER FIFTY-NINE

The Coastguard had phoned through to the Marina to say that Laura and Mia were safe and that a member of the crew was sailing the 'Christina' back.

Adam rang Jacky. 'They have found the boat, Maxwell was not on it, and Laura and Mia are safe. Where Maxwell is no one knows but the coward left his wife and daughter out at sea to fend for themselves.

Let's hope they catch up with him soon and then he will be out of Laura's life forever.'

Jacky was crying on the other end of the phone. 'Thank goodness they are ok. I can't wait to give them a hug.'

'Obviously, I will wait here until the boat arrives and then I will drive them home. They must have been terrified out there in the dark.'

'I'll be waiting for you all. Are you hungry Adam? You haven't had anything to eat for hours. Perhaps I will cook something and have it ready. I need to do something.'

'I haven't really thought about food but now you mention it, I am rather hungry.' Adam laughed.

Adam had not that long to wait. Peter Jackson was also standing beside Adam when the 'Christina' sailed back into the Marina and Mr. Jackson helped to guide it back where it was usually berthed.

Once the boat was made secure, the member of the Coastguard helped Laura down the small ladder onto the pathway. She saw Adam and immediately ran into his arms.

'Adam, how long have you been waiting here?' Laura hugged him.

The Detective said 'If it hadn't been for this young gentleman, we would never have found you so quickly. He managed to find the van that Maxwell used to kidnap you and your daughter. It led him here to the Marina.'

'Would you like to go onboard Adam and get Mia from the cabin. She has been so wonderful but has tired herself out.

Wrap her up warm in a blanket and don't forget to pick up Bunny. Maxwell stole it from the bungalow. I shudder when I think he was in there without us knowing.

Hopefully the police will soon find him.' Laura gave Adam a kiss.

Adam got on board and went down to the cabin. Mia was sound asleep. Adam carefully whispered to her to wake up.

She opened her eyes and said 'Adam, you've come to find us, I knew you would.' She put her arms around his neck and gave him a hug.

'Let's get you back on solid ground. Don't forget Bunny, he doesn't like this boat either.'

Adam picked her up and carried her off the boat and shortly afterwards, they were allowed to make their way home.

Jacky was waiting at the door of the bungalow and threw her arms around Laura and Mia.

She was crying tears of joy, so happy that her sister and niece were safe. She quickly led them indoors and made them both hot drink.

All they needed now was to hear that Maxwell had been arrested and that Laura would never have to be frightened of him ever again.

It was on the news the next day that Maxwell Hudson had been arrested by the Police and was now in custody.

At last Laura could live the life she deserved, no longer

always looking over her shoulder.

It was going to be difficult to explain to Mia about her father, but Laura decided that she would wait until Mia was older. She didn't want Mia's childhood to be spoilt.

The newspapers all wanted to print the story of how Maxwell had murdered his first wife and the owner of the boat 'Christina'.

The story of how Laura had managed to waken the people on the shore and how brave she and her little girl had been, was on the television news.

Adam was also praised for finding the van that led him and the police to the Marina.

Maxwell appeared in court and was accused of the murder of his first wife and the murder of Mr. Richard Burrows.

WHAT HAPPENED NEXT

Maxwell Hudson stood trial for the murder of his first wife Julia, was found guilty and sentenced to life imprisonment.

Mr. Colin Burton was able to give his daughter a decent burial next to her mother's grave.

Maxwell also stood trial for the murder of Mr. Richard Burrows and found guilty, was sentenced to another life imprisonment. The Judge decreed that Maxwell would be in prison for the rest of his life and would never be allowed out on parole.

Maxwell was also found guilty of the abduction of Laura and Mia and for putting their lives at risk leaving them on the 'Christina' out at sea.

Laura was at last able to divorce her husband. She was

awarded compensation for cruelty and endangering the lives of both her and her daughter.

The marital home and all the contents were sold and any money that was in Maxwell's bank accounts were deposited in Laura's bank account. The offshore bank accounts were never found, although Maxwell obviously knew where they were.

The houses in Blackwell Road, were transferred into Laura's name. She discussed with Adam what she intended to do with them. There was no way she could be happy to leave them in the disgusting state that the poor people were living in.

She decided to move the families into temporary accommodation, while the houses were completely refurbished and made safe. When the families were moved back, Laura asked for only a small rent to cover such things as Maintenance and Insurance.

She became quite a celebrity in the town and when any of the other houses in Blackwell Road came up for sale, she would buy them, and when they were refurbished, Blackwell Road became a lovely place to live.

She would contact the Council and find out who was on the waiting list to be re-housed, then she would offer them one of the newly refurbished houses. She was determined to make up for the appalling conditions that the people renting the houses from Maxwell, had endured.

Laura however, wanted to continue living in the bungalow that Auntie Mabel had left to both her and her sister Jacky.

With some of the money from the sale of the marital home, Laura asked Jacky if she would like her to build an extension on the back of the bungalow so that Jacky could live with Adam and her. Jacky already owned half the bungalow, but she didn't want to move either, so the extension was built.

Adam formally proposed once Laura's divorce came through and they decided to have a wonderful white wedding. She invited Tracy from the Estate Agents and some of her old friends that she hadn't seen for years.

The Police gave her a copy of her family tree and told her that Maxwell had visited her cousin, Mr. Charles Mortimer, and forced his way into Mr. Mortimer's house.

Laura got in touch with him and apologized for Maxwell's behaviour and said she would like to get to know him. She then invited him and his husband to her wedding.

Adam made sure that John Haynes had the exclusive photographs of their wedding for his newspaper, finally John had the romantic ending he had dreamed of printing on his front page.

Jacky was chief bridesmaid, and Mia was flower girl and bridesmaid. A year later, Adam and Laura had a baby son, a little brother for Mia to play with.

Adam decided to tell their story, so he wrote a book called 'Finding Laura' which became a best-seller and there was talk of a film being made.

With the proceeds from the book, Adam was able to leave work and pursue the career he had always dreamed of. Buying and Selling antiques.

Like all good love stories, they lived happily ever after.

THE END

ABOUT THE AUTHOR

My parents were on the stage. My father Jack E Raymond was a comedian and had a beautiful singing voice. My mother, Joan Andre, that was her stage name, was a dancer,

When my sister and I were little girls, we travelled with my parents, mainly in Scotland. We would stand in the wings and watch my father on stage, playing Dame in a pantomime. We didn't think it was strange that our father was wearing a dress!

Sadly, towards the end on the 50's and early 60's, television arrived, and the Theatres began to close as people would rather stay at home for the entertainment on the TV.

Eventually, my father and mother had to retire. It was rather sad as I knew how much they enjoyed entertaining people.

I inherited my father's singing voice and at the age of fifteen, I won a Scholarship to the Guildhall School of Music in London.

I couldn't start to train there until I was eighteen and I began to wonder if the stage was the life that I wanted to live.

I decided that travelling around the country and not knowing when the next show or concert would be, was not for me, so I declined the offer.

Sometimes I wonder whether I did the right thing, but I don't think that I was dedicated enough. I loved to sing but mainly for my own pleasure. I still did concerts and entered Music Festivals but only as an amateur.

I wrote my first book when I was about nine years old. Our teacher gave us an essay to write about a light house and I filled an exercise book. The teacher called me to the front of the class every week to read the next chapter.

My first published novel in 2019, 'The Last Waltz' was well received and has five-star reviews.

'Finding Laura' has taken me eighteen months to write and has been a help during lock downs to escape to an entirely different world for a few hours.

It is a completely different type of book to the first novel, and I found some of the details rather difficult. Luckily my son Graham helped me with the research.

I hope, Dear Reader, that you enjoy this story of Good versus Evil.

Yours sincerely

P. R. Hollywood.

Printed in Great Britain
by Amazon